Suzanne Bennett

Wells Tower's short stories and journalism have
appeared in *The New Yorker*, *Harper's Magazine*,
McSweeney's, *GQ*, *The Paris Review*, *The Anchor Book
of New American Short Stories*, *The Washington Post
Magazine*, and elsewhere. He received the Plimpton
Prize from *The Paris Review* and two Pushcart Prizes.
He divides his time between Chapel Hill, North Car-
olina, and Brooklyn, New York. *Everything Ravaged,
Everything Burned* is his first book.

Praise for *Everything Ravaged, Everything Burned*

"Remarkable . . . Tower's syntax, though always easy to follow, is supple enough to wrap itself around several shades of meaning in the same sentence. His understanding of previously under-recognized feelings is rich in detail and passionate in utterance. And his familiarity with the whole ghastly world of malls and 'cute' commercial culture is serious, even plangent, certainly not merely satirical. . . . His range is wide and his language impeccable, never strained or fussy. His grasp of human psychology is fresh and un-Freudianizing. . . . His dialogue is as crisp and contemporary and offbeat as Lorrie Moore's."
—Edmund White, *The New York Times Book Review*

"A sparkling debut . . . Tower's language is so precise, so funny . . . His ability to hint at things below the surface accounts for the immense joy these stories bring. . . . I can't tell if these stories are tragic or comic, but what makes Tower's writing so impressive is that in all cases it insists on the both/and instead of the either/or."
—Andrew Ervin, *The Miami Herald*

"Tower is a painstaking stylist devoted to the near-impossible art of polished colloquialism."   —Sam Anderson, *New York* magazine

"We need books like *Everything Ravaged, Everything Burned*."
—Benjamin Alsup, *Esquire*

"Like paper airplanes loosed from a height, the lives in *Everything Ravaged, Everything Burned* mostly spiral and crash. The art, and in the best of them it is considerable, is in the float, the impromptu curvet, the exhilarating lift on the way down."   —Richard Eder, *The Boston Globe*

"Tower's stories [have] the kind of torque that's so damnably rare these days in American short fiction, where the payoff tends to be the faint, jewel-box click of epiphany, the small tilting of a life. Tower's ambition is greater and brawnier than that."   —Jonathan Miles, *Men's Journal*

"Wonderful . . . The stories live and breathe with purpose. . . . The range and subtlety of emotional tonalities are stunning. . . . Tower has a wonderful feel for the integrity of a story, what it needs to consist of. The stories are controlled, powerful dynamisms, and they live on after one has put the book down, and expand in one's mind, and keep on expanding."   —Deborah Eisenberg, *The New York Review of Books*

"One of the most powerful and entertaining books you're likely to come across this year . . . the author's families and hapless men are bent and broken in a multitude of surprising and delightful ways."
                                                              —*Paste Magazine*

"Told with equal parts expansive charm and bitter comedy, Tower's debut story collection explores the restless terrain of middle America [and] the brutal humor inherent in it all."
                                        —Melissa Albert, *Time Out Chicago*

"Bittersweet, beautiful, and ardently conflicted . . . As evidenced by the emotional punch packed into such brief tales, Tower is almost incapable of overloading a sentence with an unnecessary word."
                                              —Kevin Canfield, *Bookforum*

"A visceral debut . . . Tower is a burgeoning master of articulating the weird shapes our private fears take when they become public—or real."
                                            —Zach Baron, *The Village Voice*

"These are lurid, ingenious, beautiful, delicate, and very funny stories. Full of pity and terror, they are also great fun to read. Wells Tower has written a brilliant book."   —Benjamin Kunkel, author of *Indecision*

"Tower routinely brings combustible materials together and has fun watching them ignite."   —Tim Adams, *The Observer* (London)

"Wells Tower is a blindingly brilliant writer who does more than raise the bar for debut fiction: he hurls it into space. With the oversized heart of George Saunders, the demon tongue of Barry Hannah, and his very own conjuring tools that cannot here be named, Tower writes stories of aching beauty that are as crushingly funny and sad as any on the planet."
                              —Ben Marcus, author of *Notable American Women*
                                              and *The Age of Wire and String*

Everything Ravaged, Everything Burned

Wells Tower

EVERYTHING RAVAGED, EVERYTHING BURNED

Picador
Farrar, Straus and Giroux
New York

FOR MY BROTHERS: DAN, LAKE, AND JOE

Contents

THE
BROWN
COAST

Bob Munroe woke up on his face. His jaw hurt and morning birds were yelling and there was real discomfort in his underpants. He'd come in late, his spine throbbing from the bus ride down, and he had stretched out on the floor with a late dinner of two bricks of saltines. Now cracker bits were all over him—under his bare chest, stuck in the sweaty creases of his elbows and his neck, and the biggest and worst of them he could feel lodged deep into his buttock crack, like a flint arrowhead somebody had shot in there. Yet Bob found that he could not fetch out the crumb. He had slept wrong on his arms, and they'd gone numb. He tried to move them, and it was like trying to push a coin with your mind. Waking up for the first time in this empty house, Bob felt the day beginning to settle on him. He shuddered at the cool linoleum against his cheek, and he sensed that not far below, not too far down in the sandy soil, death was reaching up for him.

But the little gears inside him did finally turn and haul him to his feet. He leaned against the wall to let a head rush pass, scratched the crumb from his behind, and then he went to the kitchen. He opened the refrigerator, which was empty and breathed out a sour-thermos smell. Shrunken ice cubes lay in trays in the freezer, and Bob popped one out and stuck it in his mouth. It tasted like old laundry. He spat it into the dusty cranny between the fridge and the stove.

Outside the kitchen door was the patio Bob was supposed to be down here tearing up. Thistle and rumpus weed stuck through the holes in the bricks. A table and chairs of mildewed white plastic sat canted over on high swells where tree roots were heaving up. It made him a little sick to look at that mess and think of what it would take to get it in order.

This house had once been the joint property of his father and his uncle Randall, who was wasting no time putting it on the market now that Bob's father was dead. It was an investment his father had been railroaded into six years ago, sight unseen, and Bob couldn't recall his father coming down here more than once or twice. The way the deed worked out, the place went straight to Randall, and Bob wondered whether his uncle, sixteen years Bob's father's junior, hadn't been banking on this turn of events all along.

Randall lived where Bob lived, several hours north. When Bob's father was dying, Randall had made a promise that he'd do what he could to make sure things turned out all right for his nephew. In the weeks after the funeral, Randall had made a point of stopping by frequently to condole with him, though his sympathies usually took the form of showing up around dinnertime and staying long enough to finish off whatever beers Bob had in the icebox. There was something disquieting about Randall, how his oiled hair always showed the furrows of a recent combing and how he wore braces on his teeth, though he was pushing fifty.

Bob had not been close with his father, so it was puzzling for him and also for his wife, Vicky, when his father's death touched off in him an angry lassitude that curdled his enthusiasm for work and married life. He had fallen into a bad condition and, in addition to several minor miscalculations, he'd perpetrated three major fuckups that would be a long time in smoothing over. He'd reported to work with a blind hangover, committed a calamitous oversight on a house he'd been helping to build, and soon after lost his job. A few weeks later, he'd rear-ended a local attorney, who, as a result of the collision, developed a clicking in his jaw and convinced a jury that the injury was worth $38,000, which was $2,000 more than what Bob's father had left him. Worst of all, he had tried to find relief from the unpleasantness by trysting with a lonely woman he'd met in traffic school. There'd been no joy in it, just a two-week spate of drab skirmishes in a basement apartment that smelled heavily of cat musk.

Not long after the affair had run its course, Bob and his wife were driving into town when Vicky looked up and saw the phantom outline of a woman's footprint on the windshield over the glove box. She slipped her sandal off, saw that the print did not match her own, and told Bob that he was no longer welcome in their home.

Bob spent a month on Randall's couch before Randall got the idea to send him south. "Hole up at the beach house for a while," Randall had said. "This damn thing's just a bump in the road. You need a little time to recombobulate is all."

Bob did not want to go. Vicky was already beginning to soften on her demands for a divorce, and he was sure that with time she'd open her door to him again. But Vicky encouraged him to leave, and things being how they were, he thought it best to oblige her. Anyway, it was a generous offer on Randall's part, though Bob was not surprised that when Randall dropped him off at the bus station, he'd handed him a list of jobs already written out.

Randall's house was not a delightful place—a cinder-block cottage with flaking pink paint. The sallow linoleum that covered the living room floor had been improperly glued and was coming loose, curling back on itself at a long seam running the length of the room. The wood paneling in the living room had shrugged up over many moist summers, and now the walls looked like a relief map of unfriendly, mountainous land. "Lvn rm/Sheet-Rock!" it said in the note.

In the windowless hall, Randall had hung the taxidermied bodies of some things he'd killed. An armadillo. An alligator's head with a deer's face sticking out of its mouth, his uncle's idea of wit. A square of plywood showcasing a row of withered turkey beards. Above the kitchen sink was a painting of a beer can with Randall's signature in the bottom right corner. Randall had done a good job with the Budweiser script, but he'd had to stretch out the can's midsection to accommodate all the letters, so it bulged in the middle, like a snake swallowing a rat.

In a dark corner of the living room, an old aquarium burbled away. It was huge—as long as a casket and three feet deep—and empty except for a bottle of hair tonic, a waterlogged bat corpse, and some other things floating on the surface. The water was thick and murky, the color of moss, but still the aerator breathed a steady green sigh of bubbles through the tank. Bob clicked it off. Then he stepped into his flip-flops and went outside.

He crossed the cockeyed patio. Tiny lizards scattered from his path. He followed the sound of waves to the end of the yard, through a stand of pine trees, limbless and spectral. He stepped from the pines onto a road paved with oyster shells whose brightness in the morning light made his eyes clench up.

The house was at the northern tip of a small island, and it had given Bob a little jolt of hope and excitement when Randall had described the place to him. He liked beaches, how each day the tide scoured the sand and left it clean, how people generally came to the coast because they wanted to have a good time. But when Bob reached the access path up by the bridge, he was crestfallen to see that this island did not seem to have any beach at all. The land here met the water in a steeply sloping apron of mud that sang with mosquitoes and smelled terribly of fart gas. The nearest decent beach, a man on the bus had warned him, was on another island three miles out to sea and cost twelve dollars to get to on a boat. Still, he thought it might be nice to get in that water, but in this particular spot, he'd have to climb back over the muck and walk home covered in filth. He turned around and headed back down the lane.

A pair of white-haired women in a yellow golf cart rolled past. "Hidy," one of them said to Bob.

"All right, now," he said.

Right then the sound of metal on metal rose in the lane, along with a man's voice raised in rage. "Son of a bitch!" The voice belonged to a man bent down half-vanished under the hood of a Pontiac. "Aw, God fuck a milk cow!" The white-haired women turned pursed faces at the angry man. The golf cart whined and moved faster but not much.

The jazz of oaths kept coming loud, and the birds fell silent at the din. The man's anger, Bob found, was getting him angry, too. It occurred to him to go and yank the sawed-off broom handle that was holding up the Pontiac's hood, but he did not. He walked over and stood beside the man.

"Hey, come on, man," Bob said. "There's people out here besides you."

The man pulled his head out of the hood and stared at Bob. His face was nearly all cheek, with small, crooked features that looked like they'd been stuck on in a hurry. He held a little pry bar in his hand.

"Who the fuck are you?" the man asked in a tone more mystified than hostile.

"Bob," Bob said. "I'm staying over there."

"At Randall Munroe's? I know Randall. I did a couple of things to his cat."

Bob squinted. "Do what?"

"Derrick Treat. I'm a veterinarian."

"I didn't mistake you for a car mechanic," Bob said.

"Took me three hours to get this alternator in here. Now I find out it won't take the goddamn belt."

Bob knew a couple of things about cars, and he had a look at the problem, which was easy enough to remedy. Derrick hadn't positioned the tensioner correctly before torquing down the pivot bolt. Bob made the adjustment, and the belt slipped snugly into the pulley groove. But the car still wouldn't crank because the battery was dead, so Bob had to kick off his flip-flops and jog down the lane, hunching and straining at the Pontiac's bumper to work up the speed for a roll-start. Finally, the engine caught and the car spurted off, leaving Bob gasping in the road with a mouthful of exhaust.

Derrick turned the car around. He pulled alongside Bob. He revved the engine into the high red, working his lips to mimic the shriek of the motor.

He held some money out the window. "Here, goddammit. Here's five dollars. Wait, I got seven."

"I won't take that money."

"Go on," said Derrick. "You saved my entire day."

"Turned one bolt is all I did."

"More than my dumb ass knew to do. Now come in the house and have something to cool off with at least."

Bob told him thanks, but he meant to try and find some way down to the water.

"Uh-huh, because the ocean'll dry up by the time you have one drink," Derrick said.

"Little early for me, anyhow," said Bob.

"Brother, it is one o'clock in the afternoon, and it is Saturday. Go on inside."

Turning the man down, Bob understood, was going to be a job in itself. He followed Derrick out of the sun.

The same cheap and careless people who'd built Randall's cottage had built Derrick's home, only they'd paved it in blue linoleum instead of white. The place felt lived in, at least. It smelled of fresh coffee, and it had been furnished to capacity. The small living room was jammed with a lot of false antique furniture bought as a set, all of it broken out in pediments and lathework grenades and ornamental buboes that filled every line of sight.

By the window, a woman was sitting in a recliner reading a magazine and sucking on a cigarette. She was pretty, but she'd spent too much time in the sun. She was pruned over and nearly maroon, like a turkey beard.

"Bob, this is Claire," Derrick said. "Claire, this gentleman worked some magic on our vehicle. Just went *ernh-ernh* with that ratchet, and now it'll run out from under you."

Claire smiled at Bob. "Well, that's something," she said, shaking Bob's hand and not minding the grease. "New out here?"

Bob said he was, and she told him welcome. She said he should come by anytime and that the door was always open and that she meant that.

Bob followed Derrick to the kitchen. Derrick pulled two jelly jars from the freezer along with vodka in a plastic bottle. He called to the living room. "You need a drink, baby doll?" Claire said she did, and Derrick pulled out a third jar. He poured champagne into each one and quashed the rising bubbles with the vodka, which was chilled to syrup. "Claire calls it a Polack holiday," Derrick said, handing a drink to Bob. "Her people are from over there, and they don't fool around. Drink two of them, and I've got a hangover for life, but she can knock these back all day and be fine in the morning."

They went back to the living room, and Bob sat on the sofa. Derrick sat on the arm of the recliner with his arm around Claire.

"What do you do, Bob?" Claire asked him.

"Just kind of on sabbatical, I guess," Bob said. He knocked back his drink and a sour heat bloomed in his stomach. "Probably go back to carpentering before long, what I was doing for a while."

"But what?" Claire asked.

"I built some stairs wrong and got let go. After that, I thought I'd take a little while to get a few things straightened out."

"That doesn't sound right—stairs," Claire said. "That doesn't sound like anything to get canned about."

Bob explained what it took to build a staircase, how you've got to cut each rise on the stringers exactly the same height, even a sixteenth-inch difference and people will stumble. "I don't know why, but I cut a stair in the middle to six inches instead of eight, just my brain went on the fritz. Then the old man whose house it was came by to see the job. He was going down those stairs, and wham, he fell and landed at the bottom with a broken leg. After that, a lawyer went over with a tape measure and that was it, pretty much."

"That's what I'm talking about," said Claire. "Only in America does somebody get rich off of being too dumb to walk stairs."

"I didn't feel real hot about it," said Bob. "That bone was sticking out pretty good."

Claire shrugged with her face. "Even so."

He drained the jar and set it on the table. "Well, thanks for this," he said. "Guess I better push on."

"Look, now you just got here," Derrick said, but the phone rang in the kitchen and Derrick went after it. Claire dipped a finger in her drink and then stuck the finger in her mouth. A saw-edged scar ran down the back of her hand, standing out pink and tender on the skin there, which was the color of a pot roast.

"You should stick around and have some brunch," she said. "I'm making eggs and salmon cakes."

Derrick came back from the kitchen, talking into a cordless phone, his voice loud with expertise. "Say what? Did you take a look? Can you see the head? Uh-huh. Red or whitish? Yeah, that's natural. Sounds like she's getting ready to domino. I'll be over."

Derrick came back into the living room. "Gotta take a ride over the bridge," he said. "Need to go pull something out of a horse's pussy."

"What kind of a thing?" Bob asked.

"A baby horse, I hope."

Before he left, Derrick showed Bob where to cut across the yard to get down to the sea. It was much hotter now, and the sun glared down through the gray sky like a flashlight behind a sheet. Bob walked across a dead garden and through a salt-burned hedge that rattled as he passed. He slapped along in his flip-flops, woozy from that drink and with a heat headache coming on. At the top of a steep bank of dunes, he stopped and saw the sea. The water lay in bands of blue and green, patterned over with little wind divots like a giant plate of hammered copper. At the foot of the slope, a long tongue of smooth rock stretched a couple of hundred feet into the waves.

Bob started going down the dune, but it was steep here, too, and the simplest thing was to ride down it on your ass. When he got to the bottom he had grit in his shorts and skeins of shore weeds looped between his toes.

He scrambled along the spit of rock. The wind cut the stagnant dampness of the day and dried the sweat on his face and chest. He took the salt into his lungs and savored the pure itch in his chest. He touched the long grasses waving in the water like women's hair. He crouched to observe the barnacles, their tiny feathery hands combing blindly for invisible prey.

Not far from the water's edge, Bob nearly put his foot into a deep tide pool in the rock. It was big as a bathtub and deeper than he could see. A pair of crimson starfish clung to the edge. He fished them out. They were hard and spiny in his hands, but they were nice to look at, and he thought he might nail them up somewhere for an ornament, so he dropped them into the stretched-out belly of his T-shirt. He was about to move on, when he saw something moving in the blue deeps of the hole — a fish, four pounds at least, and gorgeous, nearly the same dark blue as the water, just sitting there, gently working its bright yellow fins. It was a fish for looking at, not eating, a kind of fish that would cost you good money at a pet store. Bob dropped the starfish on the rock. He crouched beside the hole and put his hands in the water. The fish didn't move, even when he reached his fingers down beside it, but when he snatched for it, the fish darted to the far side of the hole but then just sat there, idly finning.

He crept after the fish, taking an easterly circuit around the hole so he wouldn't cast a shadow on the pool. Again he put a hand in the water, but he didn't do a big grab right off. With his left arm, he braced himself against the edge of the hole and, leaning over, let a string of spit unwind off his lip. The white bead hit the water; the pretty fish perked up. After a moment's contemplation, it floated over and ate the spit. Bob supposed the fish was starving in that hole, which explained its listlessness and the expectant way it now hovered just below the surface, waiting for another bit of lunch to fall out of the sky. Bob spat again, and the greedy fish lipped it up. Then he hocked up a lush wad from the back of his throat and lowered it toward the water on a slow strand. The fish sat rapt and waiting. As the gob neared the surface, Bob slipped a hand beneath the placid fish, lunged, and, to his own astonishment, flipped it out of the hole. It jerked and bounced across the rock, and Bob felt a panic shoot through him. He tore his T-shirt off, dipped it in the water, and draped it on the flopping fish in a shroud. Then he sprinted up the dune with the swaddled fish buckling and writhing against his chest. It was a violent and vital sensation, and Bob wondered for a moment if it was anything like this when a woman had a baby inside her.

Bob ran across Derrick's yard. Claire was in a bikini on the concrete porch. She waved to him and he yelled hey but didn't stop. He ran with his flip-flops in his fingers and cursed the oyster shells under his feet.

He made it back to the house, busted open the screen door, and dumped the fish into the aquarium. It sank and then slowly floated to the surface, fixing Bob with a vacant eye.

"Uh-uh. No way, buddy," Bob told the fish with stern pity.

He placed his palm beneath it and swept the foul water through its gills, and soon it stirred again. He pulled out the bottle of hair tonic and the bat and dropped them on the floor. The fish, which had lost part of its delicate tailfin on the rocks, drifted indifferently to one end of the tank and nibbled at a pencil that was standing in the corner.

Using a tin saucepan as a ladle, Bob bailed out most of the old green water, leaving just enough to keep the fish covered. He cleaned out the rest of the junk: bottle caps, a doll's head, and almost three dollars in change. Then he got a soup pot from the kitchen and ferried up clean water from the sea. It took him forty-five minutes, toting the sloshing pot uphill and going back for more, but when the aquarium was full Bob stood back and beheld it, gratified.

The fish swam in contented circles and did not seem to mind the tiny white crabs that had come in with the seawater. The seams were sweating a little, and Bob patched them as best he could with caulk he found under the sink. Then he hiked over to the grocery store and bought two kinds of fish food. He carried it back, and sprinkled a little pinch of each into the tank to see which one the fish preferred.

That night he borrowed a folding cot from Derrick and Claire and set it up in the living room. He put a lamp behind the aquarium and turned it on. He did not like it in this house, its odors of old meals, how the place hummed with the shrill tunes of insects that breezed in through the unscreened windows. Lying there waiting for sleep to come, Bob found some calm in the sight of his fish, so large and placid, hanging there in the glowing water. For a while, it slowly patrolled the glass and peered out at Bob with a large, gold-rimmed eye. Then all of a sudden it stopped in the middle of the tank, shivered, and began blowing from its mouth a translucent, milky sac. Bob sat up in the cot and watched the fish with awe. The sac trembled in the water but held its form. When it had grown to the size of a basketball, the fish glided inside and seemed to fall asleep.

In the morning Bob went out to the patio. It was beyond hope. Even to weed it wasn't half worth the little money Randall had vaguely promised, and he'd be damned if he'd rip up those bricks and fix the grade as the note instructed. Still, he guessed he could pull a weed or two, if only to justify a long afternoon down on the shore watching the waves come in.

The work made him angry, first at Randall, who it was obvious hadn't so much as dragged a broom across this patio in the six years he'd owned it, and then at himself, for letting his life drift back to a place where he'd had to take the kind of ape work he had not done in years. Bob had helped build five whole homes, from the mudsills to the shingles. He'd put up a house for himself and Vicky, and when she first saw it finished, she couldn't stop laughing because it looked so good. What a gentle, decent kind of life he'd had with her. What a perfect pageant of disgrace he'd cast himself in now: down on all fours, clawing like an animal at thorns and marsh cherries whose yellow fruit left his hands smelling like bad breath, the red weight of the sun on him, and nobody around to pity his cracked hands or bring him something cool to drink.

With all the weeds gone, the patio did not look good. It was tidy, but now the big swells where the tree roots lay were easier and more unpleasant to see. The sight seemed an insult to the work he'd already done. Despite himself, he started on the bricks. When he'd pulled and stacked them, he set upon the roots below, snatching at the young pale ones with his bare hands and chopping at the stout pine roots with Randall's rusty ax. It took the rest of the day, and by the time Bob knocked off in the afternoon he was aching and had a raw sunburn on his face and arms. He went inside and mixed up some old Kool-Aid, which hardly masked the sulfurous bite of the water that ran from the tap. Then he walked down toward the shore, and he brought the soup pot with him.

Derrick was out in his yard, and Bob wished he'd cut through the bushes on the other side of Derrick's house. But Derrick got out of his chair and waved Bob over. He had on a green plastic visor and a pair of the tiniest jean shorts that Bob had ever seen on a man. "Hey, man," Derrick said. "What're you doing?"

"I thought I'd go get my feet wet," Bob said. "I've been working like a slave all day."

"Doing what?"

"Picking shit up and putting shit down."

"Sounds nice," said Derrick. "I was up at five this morning throwing a purse-string suture on a hog with a prolapsed butt hole. What's that boil pot for?"

"I dunno," Bob said. "I was maybe going to put some sea life in it."

"Huh. Hold up a second." Derrick went into the house and came back out carrying a faded green dip net with an aluminum handle. "Here you go. I'll come down with you, if you don't mind."

Bob shrugged.

They skitched down the dune and got out on the spit. The sun looked orange and slick, like a canned peach. Bob dipped a foot in the mild water.

"I'm getting in," Bob said, unbuckling his belt.

Derrick was brushing off a spot on the rock and was slowly getting down on it. "In the water? To swim?" Derrick asked.

"Yes," Bob said. He shucked his shorts and waded in.

"What, nude?"

Bob didn't answer. He pushed out into the water, which was

thick and warm as baby oil. Even when he stopped moving, the water buoyed him up and wouldn't let him sink.

"All right," Derrick said. "But don't laugh at my small pecker."

He took his pants down. Bob glimpsed the melancholy little change purse he had between his legs, and looked away. Derrick's problem. Bob didn't want to know about it. He stroked into the tide.

The sea floor dropped away fast, and just a few feet out, his feet couldn't reach the bottom. He dived down through the green water and floated for a moment in the mantle of coolness where the sun's heat didn't reach. That would be an all right place to stay, if you could only find a way to linger there. But his lungs were full of air, and he soon felt the surface break across his back.

Claire was picking her way down through the grass. She wore a terry-cloth skirt and a leopard print bikini top. She waved to Bob.

"Back up, Claire," Derrick called out. "Bob is a nudist, and he's got me involved in it."

"I see," said Claire. Bold as an athlete, she shrugged off her top and pushed her skirt down. Across her breasts and oval hips, her skin looked soft and new and pale as paraffin. Bob floated off the tip of the spit, looking at her and smoothing the water with his sore hands. He watched her ease into the green curl.

He considered for a moment the many miles that lay between him and his own wife, and what it would take to cinch that distance up again. A lot of talking, a lot of work was what it would take, more than a hundred patios. It was a discouraging thought, and Bob slipped beneath the water with the weight of it.

With the sun beginning to sag, Bob crawled out and got his shorts back on. Derrick and Claire were still far out in the waves, their heads blinking in and out of sight as the swells fell and rose.

He went to the hole in the rock and saw that the last tide had filled it with amazing things. A quivering halo of vermilion minnows hung near the surface. Hugging the side of the rock was a little blue octopus no bigger than a child's hand, advancing on a yellow snail. Bob got the net. The minnows slipped through the mesh easily, but when Bob went for the octopus, it panicked and pushed off straight into the netting. He dropped it into the pot, and then plucked the snail with his fingers.

Derrick climbed out of the water and came and had a look. "Caribbean reef octopus," he said. "They mostly live south of here, but when the water starts going through its cooling, like it is right now, the current goes a little haywire and draws these funny drifts up here."

A smoky curtain of squalls was moving in from the west. Claire crawled out of the water, catching her balance in a long-legged sprinter's crouch so as not to scrape a knee. Then she stooped and braceleted a dark thigh with her fingers, easing her hand down the length of her leg, stripping the water off in silver peels. Bob watched her dry the second leg this way, and the beauty of it made his throat itch. While Derrick went on about wildlife and currents, Bob coughed into his fist.

"Also, there's Harlan's Ridge, a little underwater mountain range about a mile out that way. It splits some of the Gulf Stream off and shoots a little splinter of it at our cove, and a lot of wild things come in with that, year round. Eagle rays, turtles, scorpion fish, just strays and accidentals, stuff that don't belong here."

Claire put a hand on Derrick's shoulder. She licked away the beads of seawater caught in the bleached down on her upper lip.

"Remember last year, that dorado?" Claire said.

"Dolphin," said Derrick. "Now, that's a deep-sea fish, but there it was, about yay long. We boiled it in coconut milk. Buddy, I've probably ate a thousand dollars' worth of shit out of this hole over the years, no joke. What you got down there is a deep cave. A while back I dropped a forty-foot— Now look—"

He broke off and took the net from Bob. A khaki eel about eighteen inches long had appeared on the far side of the pool. On tiptoes, Derrick crept to where the eel lay and hauled it out with a quick jab of the net.

"*Anguilla rostrata*," said Derrick. "American eel. It's a little puny, but we could put him on the grill."

"No, uh-uh," Bob said. "Give it here. I want to keep it."

"You know the thing about these?" Derrick said, still holding up the netted eel. "These and European eels, they both start out as babies in the Sargasso Sea. Some ride the Gulf Stream up this way and some cruise all the way to Europe. Same eel, it's just where you catch it."

While Derrick was talking, the eel struggled over the hoop and started wriggling fast for the water. Derrick scrambled after it. He ushered the creature back into the net with his hand, and in the process, the eel bit him hard on the thumb. Cursing, Derrick slung it into the pot.

"You just lost the rights on that motherfucker, Bob," Derrick said, sucking his nail. "He's got an appointment with some hot coals."

But Bob picked up the pot and carried it up the slope.

The week wore on and Bob fell into a good rhythm, working in the days, jawing with the neighbors on evenings when he felt like it, spending time down by the water when he did not. He brought back many things for the aquarium: a hermit crab, sea horses, a small dogfish. One day he and Derrick rode the Pontiac to a pier down the coast and caught hardhead catfish on pork rind bottom rigs. They took the fish back to Randall's house, and Claire came over. When she saw Bob's aquarium she put her hand to her mouth and said she couldn't believe he'd hauled all of that stuff out of the sea. Then she gathered the catfish to clean them. As a child, she said, her father always made her dress the catch. She'd hated the chore back then, but she found satisfaction in it now.

Out in the yard, Bob watched her nail the fishes' heads to a piece of plywood and then douse them in boiling water from the kettle. She made a couple of slits with a box knife, and with a special pair of pliers, she peeled the skin down, neat as a whistle, revealing the snowy flesh beneath. She cut the fish into bite-size cubes, dipped them in store-bought breader, and dropped them into a pan of boiling oil.

They sat on the patio and ate off paper plates.

"Look at you, Bob, this is pretty work you did out here," Claire said, surveying how he'd done the bricks. She was on her fourth beer and there wasn't much warmth in her voice. "I'd like to get you over and handyman up a few things for me. I'd like to get a front door with a window in it, and maybe a couple of cheap skylights. Though if we were smart people, we'd probably just light that piece of shit on fire and start from scratch."

"Why say that, Claire?" said Derrick. "We're having a good time, and then you have to say something like that."

"Well, it's the truth," said Claire.

Bob didn't care to hear any of this. He pulled a tiny bone from his lips and flicked it into the dark yard. "I'll probably split in a couple of days," he said. "Maybe you'll look after those fish in there when I'm gone."

The next night he walked to the store in the island's little village and called home on the pay phone. A big halide bulb buzzed at the top of the telephone pole, and a confetti of moths bumped and tumbled in the yellow glare. He plunked a handful of quarters into the slot. For a moment he waited. A man picked up.

"Hey, Randall," Bob said.

"Buddy," Randall said. "What's the word?"

"I don't know," Bob said. "I fixed your patio. Slapped some paint on those cabinets, too."

"Thank you, my man. That's a lifesaver. Would've done it myself, but you know . . . Anyhow, that's great." There was a pause, and then Randall sneezed into the phone. "How's that paneling looking?"

"It's looking pretty fucked-up, which is how it's gonna stay," Bob said. "I don't intend to hump a bunch of Sheetrock back from the store in a wheelbarrow."

"You can't get hold of a truck or something? Rent one?" Randall said. "Or maybe they deliver. Hell, I don't know, Bob, figure it out."

"What are you up to in my house?" Bob said.

Bob heard Randall saying something that he couldn't make out. Vicky got on and said hello.

"Hey, Vick," he said.

"Well, how is it?"

"Oh, real great," Bob said. "I struck oil in the yard. It's all champagne and gold toilets down here. I got people on call to put grapes in my mouth. But, anyway, I've enjoyed it about all I can. I'm getting ready to get ready to come on back."

"Huh," she said. "We have to talk about some things."

Bob asked what things, and Vicky didn't say at first. She told him that she loved him and that she spent a lot of time worrying over him. She said she pitied him for the unwise things he'd done. She said she did not like being without him, but that, though she tried hard to, she could not think of a reason to take him back right now. In a calm, lawyerly style, she detailed a long catalog of Bob's shortcomings. From the sound of it, she had everything written down with dates and witnesses and the worst parts underlined. Bob listened to all of this and he felt himself get cold.

He watched a mouse walk out from behind the soda machine. It was eating a coupon.

"Why don't you tell me about what Randall's doing on my property," he said. "Why don't we talk about something like that?"

"How about let's talk about nothing," she said. "I'm a happier person when I forget who you are."

Bob sighed and went into a fumbling half-hearted apology, but Vicky wouldn't answer, and he suspected she was holding the phone away from her face, as he'd seen her do when her mother called. Then he retreated to the subject of his uncle, which felt like solid ground, and began to deliver some big claims about what he planned to do to him if he didn't mind his business.

"Why don't you put it in a postcard, Bob?" she said. "Hey, look, I'm about to burn some noodles here. Enjoy yourself, all right? Keep in touch."

"Now, look, goddammit," Bob said, and Vicky hung up before he could tell her any of the things he'd really called to say.

Bob walked home with the sunset nearly dead. He went past the town's one bar and heard men and women laughing. He turned at the chamber of commerce, which was just an old converted garage where they'd hung out a wooden shingle with some crooked letters burned into it instead of a sign. Past the post office, he picked up the road home and followed it into the dusk.

Bob was getting into bed when Derrick came over. He opened the door without knocking. "Oh, no," Bob said out loud.

Derrick staggered into the house on splayed legs. He squinted around the room for a long second or two before he spotted Bob sitting on the cot.

"Get up," Derrick said. "You'n me's going into town."

Bob sighed. "Man, go home," he said. "Where's Claire?"

"Fuck Claire," Derrick said. "I'm telling you, she cursed at me. She disrespected me, and she spoke to me in a manner that was atrocious. Hell with her. Now, let's ride down to Cocoa Beach and find some people to fuck and kiss."

"Sit down," said Bob. "I'll fix you a drink."

"Good idea," said Derrick.

Bob went into the kitchen and mixed up a jug of Kool-Aid and poured some into a cup. When he got back to the living room, Derrick was asleep on the floor, quietly honking in his slumber. Bob couldn't wake him, so he turned Derrick on his side, covered him with a blanket, and lay down on the cot.

Sleep had just dragged Bob down when Claire knocked, then opened the door and angled her head into the room.

"He's down there, out pretty hard," said Bob. "I shoved on him a while and couldn't get anything out of him."

She stepped in. "We can let him stay like that," she said. "I brought this thing for you."

She clicked on a lamp. She was holding a glass salad bowl filled with water. A brown speckled thing lay on the bottom. Its spongy body was studded with thorny reddish nodes; to Bob, it looked like the turd of someone who'd been eating rubies.

"What is it?" Bob asked.

"Not sure. Sea slug, I guess. Found it today," she said. "It's ugly as death, isn't it? Maybe it'd at least make the other fish feel good about theirself. You want it?"

"All right," said Bob.

She pushed back the cover on the aquarium and dumped the thing in. Then she padded over to Bob's cot. "You down for the count, or do you want to hang out some?"

He slid his hand into the hollow place behind her knee and then drew it back. She knelt beside him. He reached under her hair and cupped the back of her skull, and she made a soft un-hitching noise in the back of her throat.

"You want me to get in there with you?" she said.

"Yeah, but don't," Bob said.

"Why not?"

He didn't answer. She frowned and waited for a minute. Then she turned off the lamp and lay down beside her husband on the floor.

Bob woke up early. Claire was snoring hard. The air was close and boozy with her and Derrick's breath. She was curled in the bay of Derrick's arms, holding one of his big thumbs in her fist. When Bob stirred, her eyes opened for an instant and closed again.

The sun was still low in the sky. It slanted in through the windows and washed the room in brittle light. Bob glanced at the far end of the room and saw that things were not all right with his aquarium. He couldn't see the eel or the fantastic fish with the long yellow fins. He walked over and saw that they were all floating together, making an unsteady, fleshy terrain on the surface of the tank. In the middle of the empty water was the slug-like thing Claire had brought. It stretched and flexed, floating in happy solitude behind the glass.

Bob thought he might throw up. He made a fist and drove it hard into the center of the glass. That didn't satisfy him, so he hit it twice more, putting his full weight into it. The tank rocked back and then pitched forward off the stand, hitting the floor with a wet cymbal clap. Glass flew, and dead and dying creatures washed through the room.

Claire jumped up when the wave hit her. Derrick, whose cheek had been flush against the floor, sat up and spat out a mouthful of aquarium water even before he had his eyes open all the way. Then he looked down at the crab that had fetched up on his lap, then at Bob and Claire with a question on his face that seemed to have no feasible answer. He said, "What in the hell is going on in this living room?"

Bob tried to speak but his throat was painfully dry. A periwinkle was caught beneath his toes. He reached down and pinched it between his thumb and forefinger until he heard its shell give way. The slug was lying by the baseboard, caught up in a wad of hair and lint.

"Claire, I guess your slug killed all my fish," Bob finally said, breathing hard. He went over and tipped the creature into a coffee cup.

"Fuckin' sea cucumber is what that is," said Derrick. "These things are poisonous as hell. You can't put these sonsabitches in with other fish. Wait, now, *you* brought it over here, honey?"

"Yeah, last night, but I—"

"Now dammit, Claire, why didn't you show me that fucker first? I'd've sure as shit told you—"

"It's all right," said Bob.

"No, man," said Derrick, looking at ruined creatures at his feet. "That's a crusher, just a straight crusher."

"Oh, Bob, I'm so, so sorry," Claire said. "Oh, Bob, I feel so bad."

"No big deal," Bob mumbled.

"What a wicked thing. Oh, Bob," said Claire. "Put it down the toilet."

"Pack its ass in salt. Make it pay," Derrick said.

But Bob felt a kind of kinship with the slug. Had he been born a sea creature, he doubted God would have robed him in blue and yellow fins like the splendid dead fish at his feet, or put him in the body of a shark or barracuda or any of those exquisite destroyers. No, he'd probably have been family to this sea cucumber, built in the image of sewage and cursed with a chemical belch that ruined every lovely thing that drifted near.

"Nah, I'm going to chuck it back in the sea." Holding the cup before him like a sentry with his candle, Bob went out the back door. Claire and Derrick followed him, talking about the used aquariums they had down at the St. Vincent DePaul, and how on Monday they would go down there and hook Bob up with a fifty-gallon outfit on Derrick's dime.

"Yes, we will," said Claire. "And we'll go down to Dubey's Pet World and get you all kinds of real great things, way better stuff than even what you had."

"I guess we'll see," said Bob, sounding far away.

As they reached the end of the stone jetty, they were surprised to see a catamaran sailboat swinging in from the sound side of the island, sliding through the sea oats and marsh bracken into clean, open water. A young man squatted at the rudder, a pleased and capable captain, his elbow cocked, a pink fist on his broad thigh. On the drum of black webbing stretched between the hulls, the young man's girl sat cross-legged, sipping orange juice from a short-stemmed flute. The girl wore a man's button-down shirt, yellow and knotted loosely at the sternum to show a white bikini top, brilliant in the late dawn light. The two beamed at each other in wholesome conspiracy, the look of young people having successfully escaped a dreary family holiday. When they rounded the spit, they waved ceremoniously at the trio standing there, as though Bob, Derrick, and Claire had gathered there expressly to wish the handsome couple well.

Claire and Derrick returned the smile and wagged their hands. And Bob Munroe was smiling, too, even as he dropped back his arm and, with a loose-limbed underhand stroke, lofted the slug into the blue-gold morning air. It was a good, soaring toss, and it might have dropped the creature into the pretty young woman's lap had not a surge of warm wind rolled off the land and pushed the sailboat from the shore.

RETREAT

Sometimes, sometimes, after six or so large drinks, it seems like a sane idea to call my little brother on the phone. It takes a lot of solvent to bleach out such dark memories as my ninth birthday party, when Stephen, age six, ran up behind me at the goldfish pond at Umstead Park and shoved me face-first into the murk. The water came up only to my knees, so I did some hog-on-ice staggering before completing the belly flop. My friends laughed until they wept. Our mother put Stephen across her lap and beat his calves red with the hard side of her hairbrush, which, in the eyes of my guests, only confirmed Stephen as a heroic little comedian willing to suffer for his art.

Or the time in eleventh grade, when I landed a role opposite a girl named Dodi Clark in our high school's production of *Grease*. We played a nearly invisible couple among the prancing et alia in the dance melees, and had maybe four lines between us. Dodi was a mousy girl with a weak chin and a set of extra, overlapping canine teeth. She interested me not at all, yet the sight of Dodi and me together drove Stephen into a fever of jealousy. He courted her with a siege of posters, special pens, stickers, and crystal whim-whams to throw rainbows on her windowsill. The onslaught did its job, but when Dodi finally parted her troubled mouth for Stephen's kiss, he told me years later, he balked. "Those teeth! It was like trying to kiss a sand shark. No idea why I was after her to begin with." But I know why, and he does, too: in Stephen's understanding, nothing pleasant should ever flow to me on which he hasn't exercised first dibs.

Or the spring day when I was sixteen and Stephen thirteen, and he found me in his bedroom, listening to his records. That my ears should hear the music that he adored constituted an irreparable defilement, so he gathered all the albums I'd played and, one by one, smashed them against the edge of his bureau, telling me to point out any other albums I liked so he could smash those, too.

Or the winter morning when our mother was away and I locked Stephen outside in his pajamas for a solid hour, jeering at him through the window glass while on the frozen front steps he hammered at the door, sobbing delightfully with rage. I can't explain why I did these things, except to say that I carry a little imp inside me whose ambrosia is my brother's wrath. Stephen's furies are marvels of ecstatic hatred, somehow pornographic, the equally transfixing inverse of watching people in the love act. I was still laughing when, after a chilly hour, I welcomed Stephen back indoors with a conciliatory mug of thick hot chocolate. He seized the mug with pink fingers, drained it, and then grabbed a can opener from the counter and threw it at me, gouging a two-inch gash beneath my lower lip. It left a white parenthesis in the stubble of my chin, the abiding sideways smile of the imp.

But six deep ones, and our knotty history unkinks itself into a sad and simple thing. I go wet at the eyes for my brother and swell with regret at the thirty-nine years we've spent lost to each other.

Anyhow, I started feeling that way one night in October, halfway through a fifth of Myer's Rum. I was standing on a mountain I'd recently bought in Aroostook County, Maine. In the thick of dusk, I hiked up to the peak, the air heavy with the watery sweetness of lupine, moss, and fern. Overhead, bats strafed midges in the darkening sky. I'd been here four months, but the glory of the place impressed itself on me every day. Stephen and I hadn't spoken since the spring, but tonight, with sunset still smoldering behind the molars of the Appalachian range, I felt I had more splendor than I knew what to do with. Winter would be here soon, and I wanted to hear Stephen's voice. I could just bring in a signal on the mountaintop, so I dialed him up. He answered.

"Stephen Lattimore speaking," he said. The voice itself was quiet and guarded, and poised to take offense. Three words from him were enough to put a chink in my mood.

"Stephen. Matthew."

"Matthew," he repeated, in the way you might say "cancer" after the doctor's diagnosis. "I'm with a client." Stephen makes his living as a music therapist.

"Yeah," I said. "Question for you. What's your thinking on mountains?"

There was a careful pause. From Stephen's end came the sound of someone doing violence to a tambourine.

"I have no objection to them," he finally said. "Why?"

"Well, I bought one," I said. "I'm calling you on the cell phone from the top of it."

"Congratulations," Stephen said. "Is it Popocatepetl? Or are you putting 7-Elevens on the Matterhorn?"

Over the years, I've made good money in real estate, and for reasons I can't quite figure out, this hurts Stephen's feelings. He's not a churchman, but he's extremely big on piety and sacrifice and letting you know what fine values he's got. As far as I can tell, these values consist of little more than eating ramen noodles by the case, getting laid once every fifteen years or so, and arching his back at the sight of people like me—that is, people who have amounted to something and don't smell heavily of thrift stores.

I love Stephen because he's all I've got left in the way of family. A heart attack took our father when I was ten and Stephen seven. Liquor killed our mother before I was out of college, and it was around then that we began to really drift apart. Stephen became convinced that he was going to reach great fame as a pianist, and when he wasn't practicing, he was moaning about how he should have been. He was not a large talent, but the piano offered my little brother an exit from a world he found bitter and complicated and which felt the same way about him.

I, on the other hand, have always understood that life is an as-is, no-warranty arrangement, and if you want it to add up to anything, you'd better go at it with fire in your gut. I married young, and I have married often. I bought my first piece of property at eighteen. Now, at forty-two, I've been through two amicable divorces. I've lived and profited in nine American cities. Late at night, when rest won't come and my breathing shortens with the worry that my ambition might have robbed me of some of life's traditional rewards (long closenesses, offspring, mature plantings), I take an astral tour of the hundreds of properties that have passed through my hands over the years. Contemplating the small but grateful multitude living in or banking returns off of holdings whose hidden value I was first to spy, the terror eases. Anxiety quits its bagpiper's clasp on my lungs, and I droop, contented, into sleep.

Stephen spent his inheritance on music school, where he studied composition. What I heard of his music was gloomy, the sound track you might crave in an idling car with a hose running from the tailpipe, but nothing you could hum. When no orchestras called him with commissions, he had an artistic crackup, exiled himself to Eugene, Oregon, to buff his oeuvre and eke out a living teaching the mentally substandard to achieve sanity by blowing on harmonicas. When I drove down to see him two years ago after a conference in Seattle, I found him living above a candle store in a dingy apartment that he shared with a dying collie. The animal had lost the ability to urinate, so Stephen was always having to lug her downstairs to the grassy verge beside the sidewalk. There, he'd stand astride the poor animal and manually void its bladder via a Heimlich technique horrible to witness. You hated to see your last blood relation engaged in something like that. I told Stephen that from a business standpoint, the smart thing would be to have the dog put down. This caused an ugly argument, but really, it seemed to me that someone regularly seen by the roadside hand-juicing a half-dead dog was not the man you'd run to for lessons on how to be less out-of-your-mind.

"The mountain doesn't have a name yet," I told him. "Hell, I'll name it after you. I'll call it B.A.S.S. Hill." (A family acronym: "Bald and Something Stinks." Stephen started losing his hair in his early twenties, and he has an upturned, disapproving nose, as though he's perpetually sniffing something foul.)

Stephen chuckled dryly. "Do that. Hanging up now."

"I send you any pictures of my cabin? Gets its power off a windmill. It's the absolute goddamn shit. You need to come out here and see me."

"What about Charleston? Where's Amanda?"

I spat a lime rind into my hand and tossed it up at the bats to see if they'd take a nibble at it. They didn't.

"No idea."

"You're kidding. What went wrong?" His voice took on a practiced, clinical solemnity, though the tambourine slaughter ongoing in the background diminished its effect.

There's no shame in admitting that I was in a transitional period at the moment. Like a lot of wise and respectable people, I'd been caught off guard by sudden reverses in the Charleston real estate market. I'd had to borrow some cash from my ex-fiancée, a rich woman who didn't care about money just so long as she didn't have to loan out any of hers. Strains developed and the engagement withered. I used the last of my liquidity to buy the proud hill on whose peak I was standing now. Four hundred acres, plus a cabin, nearly complete, thanks to my excellent neighbor George Tabbard, who'd also sold me the land. The only hitch was I'd have to spend a year in residence up here, but next fall I could subdivide, sell the plots, dodge the extortionary tax assessment the state charges nonresident speculators, and cruise into life's next phase with the winds of increase plumping my sails and a vacation home in the bargain.

"Nothing went wrong," I said. "She was hard of hearing and her pussy smelled. Anyway I got a beautiful piece of unspoiled America for peanuts. Come see me."

"Now's not a great time for me," he said. "Plus I can't afford the airfare. Anyway, I'm with a *client*, Matthew. Let's talk about this later."

"Fuck the airfare," I told him. "I'll pay for the flight. I want you to come see me." Actually, this wasn't an offer I'd planned to make. I'm sure Stephen had more money in the bank than I did, but his poor-mouthing worked an exasperating magic on me. I couldn't take a second of it without wanting to smack him on the head and neck with a sack of doubloons. Then he said he couldn't leave Beatrice (the collie was still alive!). Fine, I told him, if he could find the right sort of iron lung to stable her in, I'd be glad to foot the bill for that, too. He said he'd think it over. A marimba flourish swelled in the line, and Stephen hung up.

The conversation left me irritable, and I walked back to my cabin in a low mood. But I bucked up right away when I found George Tabbard on my porch, half of which was still bare joists. He was standing on a ladder, nailing a new piece of trim across the front gable. "Evening, sweetheart," he said. "Sorry to intrude. Got bored and whipped up another *objet* for you here."

Of course he wasn't intruding. We worked together on my house nearly every day, and ate dinner together nearly every night. George was in his late sixties, but we were two peas in a pod. His family had been in the area since the 1850s, but he'd gone through some wives, scattered some kids, moved around a good deal, before coming home to roost, a decade or so ago. He'd pretty much built my cabin himself, and he didn't seem to mind that I could pay him only about half what he'd have earned in town. But even more than his labor, I cherished his company, which was like a gentle narcotic. He could laugh and drink and murder whole evenings rambling about chain saws, women, and maintaining equipment, and do so in such a way that you never felt there was anything more in the world to think about than these things.

A couple of groans with his screw gun, and he'd secured the item, a four-foot battery of little wooden pom-poms, like something you'd see dangling from the ceiling of a Mexican drug dealer's sedan. I'd praised the first one he'd made, but now George had tacked his lacework fancies to every eave and soffit in sight, so that the house pretty well foamed with them. He came by with a new piece of frippery about every third day. My house was starting to resemble something you'd buy your mistress to wear for a weekend in a cheap motel. But there was no one around for my cabin to appall, so I didn't see the harm. Though it had occurred to me that I was probably stuck with this hell of curlicued whimsies until George moved or passed away.

"There we are," he said, backing away to get the effect. "Pretty sharp little booger, don't you think?"

"Knocks me out, George. Thanks."

"Now how about some backgammon?"

"Fair enough."

I went inside and fetched the set, the rum, and a quart of olives I'd bought that day. George was a brutal opponent, and the games were a pointless rout, yet we sat for many hours in the cool of the evening, drinking rum, moving the lacquered discs around the board, and spitting olive pits over the railing, where they landed quietly in the dark.

To my surprise, Stephen called me back. He said he'd like to come, so we fixed a date, two weeks later. It was an hour and twenty minutes to the village of Aiden, where the airfield was, but when George and I pulled up, Stephen's plane hadn't come in. I went into the Quonset hut they use for a terminal. A little woman with a brown bomber jacket and a bulb of gray hair sat by the radio, reading the local newspaper. I'd been in and out of this airport a dozen times, but she didn't let on that she recognized me, which seemed to be a general practice among the locals. The discourtesy was probably deliberate and, in its way, practical. Shake too many hands, and before long you'd have so many friends you couldn't pick your nose without the whole county hearing about it. Still, it depressed me to have settled in a place where the salt of the earth would have out-brusqued a Newark stevedore.

"My brother's flight was due in from Bangor at eleven," I told the woman.

"Plane's not here," she said.

"I see. Do you know where it is?"

"Bangor."

"And when's it going to arrive?"

"If I knew that, I'd be somewhere picking horses, wouldn't I?"

Then she turned back to her newspaper and brought our chat to an end. The front-page story of the *Aroostook Gazette* showed a photograph of a dead chow dog, under the headline "Mystery Animal Found Dead in Pinemont."

"Quite a mystery," I said. "'The Case of What Is Obviously a Dog.'"

"'Undetermined origin,' says here."

"It's a dog, a chow," I said.

"Undetermined," the woman said.

With time to kill, we went over to the lumberyard in Aiden, and I filled the bed of my truck with a load of decking to finish my porch. Then we went back to the airfield. Still no plane. George tried to hide his irritation, but I knew he wasn't happy to be stuck on this errand with me. He'd wanted to go gunning for deer today. George was keen to get one before the weather made hunting a misery. Loading your freezer with meat slain by your hand was evidently an unshirkable autumn rite around here, and George and I had been going out twice a week since the season opened. I'd shot the head off a bony goose at point-blank range, but other than that, we hadn't hit a thing. When I'd suggested that we go in on a side of beef or something from the butcher shop, George had acted as though I'd proposed a terrible breach of code. Fresh venison tasted better than store-bought beef, he argued. Also, you were not out big money in the common event that your freezer was sacked by the meat burglars who apparently worked the outer county.

To buck George up, I bought him lunch at a tavern in Aiden, where we ate hamburgers and drank three whiskey sours each. George didn't complain outright, though he did keep lifting his eyebrows at his watch and giving a pained sigh. Already, I felt a coursing anger at Stephen for not calling to let me know that his plane was delayed. He was the kind of person who had no qualms scuttling your entire morning if it saved him the cost of a phone call. I was brooding heavily when the bartender asked if I wanted anything else. I told him, "Yeah, tequila and cream."

"You mean a Kahlúa and cream," he said, which is what I'd meant, but between Stephen and the airport woman, I felt I'd suffered enough slights for one day. "How about you bring what I ordered?" I told him, and he got to work.

While I forced the awful mixture down, the bartender told me, sneering, that I was welcome to another, on the house.

When we rolled back by the airport, the plane had come and gone. A light rain was sifting down. Stephen was out by the gate, on the lip of a ditch, perched atop his bag with his chin on his fist. He was thinner than when I'd last seen him, and he had violet half circles under his eyes. The rain had wet him through, and what was left of his hair lay sorrowfully against his skull. His wool coat and wide-wale corduroys were as old as they were ill fitting. The wind gusted, and Stephen billowed like a poorly tarped load.

"Hey, buddy," I called out to him.

His eyes flashed at me. "What the shit, Matthew?" he said. "I just stayed up all night on a plane to spend two hours sitting in a ditch? That really happened?"

"I was here three hours ago," I said. "I had things on my plate today, Stephen. But now George is drunk and I'm half in the bag and the whole day's shot."

"Oh, good," said Stephen. "Because that's why I had them hold the plane. To inconvenience you."

"What I'm saying, asshole, is that a phone call would have been considerate."

"Call you how, shitball," Stephen spat. "You know I don't do cell phones. This is your fucking . . . region, Matthew. It didn't occur to me that you'd need special instructions on how not to leave somebody in the rain."

I wanted to point out Stephen could just as easily have waited with the radio woman in the Quonset hut, but I suspected he'd arranged himself in the ditch to present me with a picture of the utmost misery when I pulled up. He was a sad portrait. He was shivering, and his cheeks and forehead were welted over from repeated gorings by the terrible cold-weather mosquitoes they had up here. Right now, one was gorging itself on the rim of his ear, its belly glowing like a pomegranate seed in the cool white sun. I didn't swat it away for him.

"Maybe you should cry about it, Stephen," I said. "Maybe a good shit fit would make you feel better." I did some theatrical sniveling, and he went livid.

"All right, motherfucker, I'm out of here." His voice was hoarse with fury. "Been a great trip. Good to know you're still a fucking asshole, Matty. Let's do this again sometime, you prick."

He shouldered his bag and stormed off for the airfield. His tiny head and squelching shoes—it was like watching a stray duckling throw a tantrum.

The old satisfaction hit me in a wave. I jogged up behind Stephen and stripped the duffel bag from his shoulder. When he turned, I put him in a bear hug and kissed his brow.

"Get the hell off of me," he said.

"Who's an angry fellow?" I said. "Who's an angry little man?"

"I am, and you're a complete fucking bastard," he said.

"Yeah. Sucks, doesn't it? Come on. Get in the truck."

"Give me back my bag," he said. "I'm leaving."

"Ridiculous," I said, chuckling. I walked to the truck and levered the seat forward to usher Stephen into the club cab's rear compartment. When Stephen saw that we weren't alone, he stopped grasping for his bag and making departure threats. I introduced Stephen to George. Then my brother climbed in and we pulled onto the road.

"This is Granddad's gun, isn't it?" said Stephen. Hanging in my gun rack was the .300 Weatherby Magnum I'd collected from my grandfather's house years ago. It was a beautiful instrument, with a blued barrel and a tiger maple stock.

"Yep," I said, marshaling a defense for why I hadn't offered the gun to Stephen, who probably hadn't fired a rifle in fifteen years. To tell the truth, Stephen probably had a stronger claim to it than I did. As kids, we'd hunted often with our grandfather, and Stephen, without making much of it, had always been the more patient stalker and a better shot. Yet Stephen didn't make a fuss about the gun.

"Hey, by the way," he said presently. "The tab comes to eight-eighty."

"What tab?" I said.

"Eight hundred and eighty dollars," Stephen said. "That's what the flight came to, plus a sitter for Beatrice."

"Your daughter?" George asked.

"My dog," said Stephen.

"George," I said, "this is a dog that remembers where it was when JFK was shot. Stephen, are you still doing those bowel lavages on her? Actually, don't tell me. I don't need the picture in my head."

"I'd like my money," Stephen said.

"Don't get a rod-on about it, Steve. You'll get paid."

"Lovely. When?"

"Jesus fucking Christ, I'm going to pay you, Stephen," I said. "It's just I happen to be operating a fucking motor vehicle at this particular point in time."

"Sure," said Stephen. "All I'm saying is that it won't blow my mind if I go home empty-handed here."

"Oh, my God!" I roared. "Would you shut up, please? What do you want, collateral? Want to hold my watch?" I joggled the wheel a little. "Or maybe I just drive us into a fucking tree. Maybe you'd like that."

George began to laugh in a musical wheeze. "How about you two stop the car and have yourselves an old-fashioned rock fight."

I flushed. To be maneuvered into revealing this idiotic side of myself in front of George . . . My loathing for Stephen caught a fresh charge. "I'm sorry, George," I said.

"Forget it," Stephen said.

"Oh, no, Steve, let's get you squared away," I said. "George, my checkbook's in the glove box."

George made out the check, and I signed it on the steering wheel and passed it to my brother, who folded it into his pocket. "Voilà," George said. "Peace in our time."

Having been outplayed over the matter of the check, Stephen began plying George with a barrage of light and pleasant chatter. Had he lived here long? Ten years? Oh, *fantastic*, what a wonderful part of the country to retire to! He'd grown up here, too? How *wonderful* to have escaped a childhood in the exurban soul vacuum we'd been reared in. And George had gone to Syracuse? Had he heard of Nils Aughterard, the music biographer on the faculty there? Well, his book on Gershwin—

"Hey, Stephen," I broke in. "You haven't said anything about my new truck."

"What'd it cost you?"

"Best vehicle I've ever owned," I said. "V-8, five-liter. Three-and-a-half-ton towing capacity, with a carriage-welded class-four trailer hitch. Four-wheel drive, max payload package. It'll pay for itself when the snow hits."

"You're really not going back to Charleston?" he asked.

"Probably not," I said. From the back, I heard Stephen lift the lid of my cooler, and then the sharp lisp of a beer being opened.

"Pass me one of those?" I said.

"Roger that," said George.

"While you're driving?" Stephen asked.

"Yeah, while I'm fucking driving," I said.

"Don't yell at me," Stephen said.

"I'm not yelling," I said. "I'd just like one of my beers."

"Holy Christ," said George. He turned and reached into the cooler, grabbed two cans, and tossed one into my lap. "We happy now?"

"Yeah," I said.

A minute passed and Stephen spoke. "So you and Amanda, that's really off?"

"Yeah."

"Ah, well," Stephen said. "And I'd thought you were so hot on her."

Stephen had made no secret of how much he'd disliked my fiancée. She was a churchgoer, raised in a conservative household, and the last time they'd met, they'd argued over the war in

Iraq. Over dinner, Stephen had baited her into declaring that she'd like to see the Middle East bombed to a parking lot. He'd asked her how this tactic would square with "Thou shalt not kill." Amanda told him "Thou shalt not kill" was from the Old Testament, so it didn't really count.

In the rearview, I caught Stephen looking at me with pity and expectation, slavering for a few morsels about our split.

I took a tube of sunflower seeds from the dashboard and shook a long gray dose into my mouth. I cracked them with my teeth and spat the chewed hulls out the window.

"To be honest with you," I said, "I just don't see the rationale for anyone owning a vehicle that doesn't come with a carriage-welded class-four trailer hitch."

In silence, we rode through bleary rural abridgments of towns, down a narrowing vasculature of country roads, to the rilled and cratered fire trail that served as a driveway to my and George's land. High weeds stood in the earthen spine between the tire grooves, brushing the truck's undercarriage with a sound of light sleet. We passed George's handsome cedar shake cottage, I dropped the truck into four-wheel drive, and the Dodge leapt, growling, up the hill.

My home hove into view. I was ready for Stephen to bust my balls a little over George's fancy trim, but he took in the place without a word.

George ambled off to have a leak in the trees. I grabbed Stephen's duffel and led him indoors. Though my cabin's exterior was well into its late rococo phase, the interior was still close to raw. Stephen gazed around the cabin, and the squalor of the place impressed itself on me with my brother standing there. The floors were still dusty plywood. I hadn't tacked the wainscoting up yet. The drywall stopped four feet from the floor, and pink insulation lay like an autopsy patient behind the cloudy plastic sheeting. The mattress I'd been sleeping on lay askew in the center of the room.

"Feel free to do a little embellishing when you write the Christmas letter this year," I told him.

He went to the window and gazed out at the wiry expanse of leafless trees sloping down the basin of the valley. Then he turned and looked at the mattress. "Where do I sleep?" he said.

I nodded at a sleeping pad rolled up in the corner.

"You didn't tell me we'd be camping."

"Yeah, well, if it's too much of a shithole for you, I can run you back to the motor lodge."

"Of course not. It's a great place. Honestly. I was expecting a modular chalet with tiered Jacuzzis and a four-car garage. This is nice. Simple."

With the instep of my boot, I herded a pile of sawdust toward the wall, and a piece of silver solder winked from the heap. The stuff was costly. I plucked it out and put it in my pocket.

"Next time you come back, I'll strip nude and wear a barrel," I said. "You'll really be proud of me then."

"No, I'm serious. I'd kill for something like this," he said, reaching up to rub his hand along a smooth log rafter. "I mean, fuck, I'll be forty next month. I rent a two-room apartment with no bathroom sink."

"That same place?"

"Yeah," he said.

"You're kidding," I said. "What about that condo you were looking at?"

"Well, yeah, but then all this stuff with the mortgage crisis," Stephen said. "Just . . . I don't know, I didn't want to get rooked."

"Fuck, man, you should have called me. The place still on the market?"

"No."

"But that money, your Gram-Gram money? You still got it for a down payment?"

He nodded.

"Listen, you get back to Oregon, we'll find you something. Look around, send me some comps, I'll help you through it. We'll get you into a place."

Stephen gave me a guarded look, as though I'd offered him a soda and he wasn't sure I hadn't pissed in it first.

I wanted to get the porch wrapped up before dark, and I suggested that Stephen take a drink up to the summit, where I'd hung a hammock, while George and I nailed the decking down. Stephen said, actually, it might be fun to swing a hammer for an hour or two. So we unloaded the wood, and he and George got to work, while I stayed inside, slathering auburn Minwax on sheets of bead-board wainscot. Whenever I poked my head out the front door, I saw Stephen in an act of vandalism against my lumber. He'd bend every third nail and then gouge the wood with the hammer's claw trying to correct his mistake. Water would pool in those gouges and rot the boards, but he seemed to be enjoying himself, so I didn't ride him about it. Through the closed windows, I could hear George and Stephen chatting and laughing as they worked. I'd learned to tolerate long hours of silence in the months I'd been up here, to appreciate it, even. Yet it warmed me to hear voices coming from my porch, though in the back of my mind, I suspected they were laughing about me.

George and Stephen took until nightfall to get all the decking in place. When they were finished, we made our way down to the tiny pond I'd built by damming a spring behind my house. We shed our clothes and pushed off into the pond, each on his own gasping course through the exhilarating blackness of the water. "Oh, oh, oh, *God*, it feels good," cried Stephen in a voice of such carnal gratitude that I pitied him. But it was glorious, the sky and the water of a single world-ending darkness, and we levitated in it until we were as numb as the dead.

Back at the house, I cooked up a gallon or so of beef Stroganoff, seasoned as George liked it, with enough salt to make your eyes water. A run of warm nights was upon us, thanks to a benevolent spasm of the Gulf Stream, and we dined in comfort on the newly finished porch. Over the course of the meal, we put away two bottles of wine and half a fifth of gin. By the time we'd moved on to brandied coffee to go with the blueberry pie George fetched from his place, the porch was humid with bonhomie.

"Look at this," Stephen said, stomping heavily on one of the newly fastened boards. "Fuckin', I've got clients I've been working with ten years, and what've I done for them? I don't know. But spend two hours banging nails, you got something to stand on, man. Real progress. This is what I oughta do. Come out here. Live on a fuckin' hill."

"Actually, I'm glad you brought that up," I said. "How big's that nest egg you've got?"

He gave a coy shrug.

"What's it, twenty-five grand or something?"

"I guess," he said.

"Because, look, check it out," I said. "Got a proposition for you."

"Okay."

"I mean, listen, how many guys like us, like me, do you think there are out there? Ballpark figure."

"What's that mean, 'like us'?" Stephen said.

And here I began to spell out for him an idea I'd had on my mind lately, one that seemed rosiest after a wine-soaked dinner, when my gladness for the land, the stars, and the bullfrogs in my pond was at its maximum. I'd get to thinking about the sad, paunchy hordes, nightly pacing carpeted apartments from Spokane to Chattanooga, frantic for escape hatches of their own. These were the gentlemen to reach. The plan was simple. I'd advertise one-acre plots in the back pages of men's magazines, put up a few spec cabins, handle the contracting myself, build a rifle range, some snowmobile trails, maybe a little saloon on the summit. In they'd swarm, a hill of pals, a couple of million in it for me, no sweat!

"I don't know," said Stephen, helping himself to another plump dollop of brandy.

"What don't you know?" I asked him. "That twenty-five grand, and I'd put you in for an even share. You'd be getting what the other investors are getting for fifty."

"What other investors?" Stephen asked.

"Ray Lawton," I lied. "Lawton, Ed Hayes, and Dan Welsh. My point is I could let you in, even just with that twenty-five. If you could kick that twenty-five in, I'd set you up with an even share."

"No, yeah, it sounds great," Stephen said. "It's just I need to be careful with that money. That's my whole savings and everything."

"Now, goddammit, Stephen, I'm sorry but let me explain something to you. I *make* money. That's what I do," I said. "I take land, and a little bit of money, and then I turn it into lots of money. You follow me? That's what I do, and I'm good at it. What I'm asking is to basically just *hold* your twenty-five grand for a couple of months, and in return you'll be in on something that could literally change your life."

"Can't do it," he said.

"Well, all right, Stephen, what can you do? Could you go ten? Ten grand for a full share? Could you put in ten?"

"Look, Matthew—"

"Five? Three? Two thousand?"

"Look—"

"How about eight hundred, Stephen, or two hundred? Would that work for you, or would two hundred dollars break the bank?"

"Two hundred's good," he said. "Put me down for that."

"Go fuck yourself," I said.

"Matthew, come on," said George. "Cool it."

"I'm totally cool," I said.

"No, you're being a shit," said George. "And anyway, your dude ranch thing isn't worth all this wind. Never work."

"Why not?"

"First of all, the county'd never let you do it in the watershed. The ten-acre buffer—"

"I already talked to them about a variance," I said. "Wouldn't be—"

"And for another thing, I didn't move back here to get among a bunch of swinging dicks."

"No offense, George, but it's not your land we're talking about."

"I know that, Matthew," George said. "What I'm saying is, you carve this hill up and sell it out to a bunch of cocksuckers from Boston, I'd say the chance is pretty good that some night in the off-season, I'd get a few too many beers in me and I'd get it in my head to come around with a few gallons of kerosene."

George was staring at me with an irritating, stagy intensity. "Forget the kerosene, George—a hammer and nails'll do it," I said, turning and sweeping a hand at the wooden dainties on my gable. "Just sneak up some night and do a little raid with your scroll saw. Turn everybody's camp into a huge doily. That'll run them off pretty quick."

I laughed and went on laughing until my stomach muscles ached and tears beaded on my jaw. When I looked back at George, he had his lips set in a taut little dash. He was evidently vain about his scrollsaw work. I could not think what to do. I was still holding my pie plate, and without giving it much thought, I flung it into the woods. A crash followed without the rewarding tinkle of shattered crockery.

"Oh, God," I said.

"What?" said Stephen.

"Nothing," I said. "My life is on fire." Then I went into my cabin and got down on my mattress, and before long I was sleeping very well.

I woke a little after three, thirsty as a poisoned rat, but I lay paralyzed in superstition that staggering to the sink would banish sleep for good. My heart raced. I thought of my performance on the porch, then of a good thick noose creaking as it swung. I thought of Amanda, and my two ex-wives. I thought of my first car, whose engine seized because I didn't change the timing belt at 100,000 miles. I thought of how, two nights ago, I'd lost thirty dollars to George in a cribbage game. I thought of how, in the aftermath of my father's death, for reasons I couldn't recall, I stopped wearing underwear, and of a day in junior high when the cold rivet in a chair alerted me to a hole in the seat of my pants. I thought of everyone I owed money to, and everyone who owed me money. I thought of Stephen and me and the children we'd so far failed to produce, and how in the diminishing likelihood that I did find someone to smuggle my genetic material into, by the time our little one could tie his shoes, his father would be a florid fifty-year-old who would suck the innocence and joy from his child as greedily as a desert wanderer savaging a found orange.

I wanted the sun to rise, to make coffee, to go out in the woods and find George's trophy buck, to get back to spinning the blanket of mindless incident stretched ever thinner across the pit of regrets I found myself peering into most sleepless nights. But the sun was slow in coming. The montage wore on until dawn, and behind it, the soothing music of the noose, *crik-creak, crik-creak, crik-creak*.

At the first bruised light in the eastern windows, I got up. The air in the cabin was dense with cold. Stephen wasn't on the spare mattress. I put on boots, jeans, and a canvas parka, filled a thermos with hot coffee, and drove the quarter mile to George's house.

The lights were on at George's. George was doing sit-ups and Stephen was at the counter, minting waffles. A very jolly pair. The percolator was gasping away, making me feel forlorn with my plaid thermos.

"Hey, hey," I said.

"There he is," Stephen said. He explained that he'd slept on George's couch. They'd been up late at the backgammon board. He handed me a waffle, all cheer and magnanimity, on his way toward another social heist in the Dodi Clark vein.

"What do you say, George," I said, when the old man had finished his crunches. "Feel like going shooting?"

He rubbed at a fleck of pyrite in one of his chimney stones. "I suppose." He turned to Stephen. "Coming with, little brother?"

"I don't have a gun for him," I said.

"Got that .30-30 he can use," George said.

"Why not," Stephen said.

Our spot of choice was Pigeon Lake, twenty miles away. You had to boat out to the evergreen cover on the far shore. After we'd eaten, we hooked George's skiff and trailer to my trailer hitch, and went jouncing into the white fog that had settled on the road.

We dropped the boat into the water. I sat in the stern, far away from my brother, and we headed north, hugging the shore, past realms of marsh grass and humps of pink granite, which in the hard red light of morning resembled corned beef hash.

George stopped the boat at a stretch of muddy beach where he said he'd had some luck before. We beached the skiff and trudged into the tree line.

My hangover was calamitous. I felt damp, unclean, and suicidal, and couldn't concentrate on anything except the vision of a cool, smooth-sheeted bed and iced seltzer water and bitters. It was Stephen who found the first heap of deer sign, in the shadow of a pine sapling stripped orange by a rutting buck. He was thrilled with his discovery, and he scooped the droppings into his palm and carried them over to George, who sniffed the dark pebbles so avidly that for a second I thought he might eat them.

"Pretty fresh," said Stephen, who hadn't hunted since the twelfth grade.

"He probably just winded us," George said. "Good eyes, Steve."

"Yeah, I just looked down and there it was," said Stephen.

George went off to perch in a nearby stand he knew about and left the two of us alone. Stephen and I sat at adjacent trees with our guns across our laps. A loon moaned. Squirrels rasped.

"Hey, Matty," Stephen said. "I wanted to talk about last night."

"How about let's don't," I said. "I've put it out of my mind."

"No, seriously. What you were saying, about me investing out here. Maybe it's something I should think about."

"I don't know."

"I mean, not necessarily the man-campus idea or whatever. But to get a little land. George was saying he sold to you for ninety bucks an acre."

"Which is fair market price," I said.

"No, yeah, I'm sure it is. I mean, Jesus, a thousand bucks, I'd have eleven acres and still enough left to put up a cabin."

"Yeah, but what would you do? What about your work?"

"What do you do out here? I'd hunt. Chop wood. Work with my hands. Reconcile the mind-body split, you know? I'm just fucking tired, Matty. I've been pushing for twenty years. I work so goddamned hard, and what have I got? I filled out this dating thing on the computer a few weeks ago. One thing they ask you is, 'If you were an animal, what would you be?' I wrote, 'A bumblebee trying to fuck a marble.' It's true. Just grinding away at this goddamned thing that never gives back. Pointless."

"The people you've helped probably don't think so," I said.

"I'm not talking about the sessions," said Stephen. "Anybody could do that. You just march them through exercises. The composing. It's all I do, Matty. I don't go out. I don't meet people. I sit in my shitty apartment and write. I could have spent the last two decades shooting heroin and the result would be the same, except I'd have some experiences to show for it."

"You just need to develop some connections," I said. "Move down to L.A. or something. You wouldn't like it out here."

"I would," he said. "I already do. You know how long it's been since I spent a day away from my piano? Just hanging out with other people? Actually living, actually being in the moment for once?"

I lifted a haunch to let a long, low fart escape.

"That's fascinating," Stephen said. "Please go on."

A moment passed.

"I mean, shit, Stephen," I said. "Let's say you did want to buy in out here. For one thing, even just building materials—"

"Wait, shut up," he whispered, cocking an ear. He fussed with the rifle. When he managed to lever a round into the chamber, he raised the gun to his shoulder and drew a bead on the far side of the clearing.

"There's nothing there," I said.

He fired, and then charged off into the brush. I didn't go with him. My head was killing me, and if my little brother had bagged a deer on his first day out, I had no interest in a supporting role in the victory. The shot summoned George. He jogged into the clearing just as Stephen was emerging from the brush.

"Hit something, little brother?" George asked him.

"Guess not," Stephen said.

"At least you got a look," George said. "Next time." He returned to his stand without saying a word to me.

At noon, George came back empty-handed. We climbed back in the boat and went skimming across the lake. The fog had burned off and there wasn't another craft in sight. The loveliness of the day was enough to knock you down. Swallows rioted above the calm green lid of the lake. Birch trees gleamed like filaments among the dark evergreens. No planes disturbed the sky. I felt dead to it, though I did take a kind of comfort that all of this beauty was out here, persisting like mad, whether you hearkened to it or not.

George took us to another stretch of lakefront woods, where we waited three hours for some edible wildlife to appear and let itself be shot, but nothing did. The sun was sinking when we plodded back to the soggy delta where we'd tied the boat. Glancing down the beach, I spotted something that I thought at first might be a driftwood sculpture, but which sharpened under my stare into the brown serrations of a moose's rack. It was standing in the shallows upwind, its head bent to drink. Three hundred yards at least, too far for a confident shot, but I raised my rifle anyway. "Goddammit, Matthew, no," George said.

I fired twice. The moose's forelegs crumpled beneath it, and an instant later I saw the animal's head jerk as the sound of the shot reached him. The moose tried to struggle upright but fell again. The effect was of a very old person trying to pitch a heavy tent. It tried to stand, and fell, and tried, and fell, and then gave up its strivings.

We gazed at the prone creature in flat-footed amazement. Finally, George turned to me, shaking his head. "That," he said, "has got to be the goddamnedest piece of marksmanship I've ever seen."

The moose had collapsed in a foot of icy river water and had to be dragged onto firm ground before it could be dressed. Stephen and I waded out to where the moose lay, and we had to crouch and soak ourselves to get rope under its chest. The other end we looped around a tree on the bank, and then tied the rope to the stern of the skiff, using the tree as a makeshift pulley. George gunned the outboard, and Stephen and I stood calf-deep in the shallows heaving on the line. By the time we'd gotten the moose to shore, our palms were puckered and torn raw, and our boots were full of water.

With George's hunting knife, I bled the moose from the

throat, and then made a slit from the bottom of the rib cage to the jaw, revealing the gullet and a pale, corrugated column of windpipe. The scent was powerful. It brought to mind the dark, briny smell that seemed always to hang around my mother in summertime when I was a child.

George was in a rapture, giddy at how I'd put us both in six months of meat with my preposterous shot. My offense of the night before seemed to be forgiven. He took the knife from me and gingerly opened the moose's belly, careful not to puncture the intestines or the sack of his stomach. He dragged out the organs, setting aside the liver, kidneys, and pancreas. One strange hitch was the hide, which was hellish to remove. To get it loose, Stephen and I had to take turns, bracing our boots against the moose's spine, pulling at the hide while George slashed away at the fascia and connective tissues. I saw Stephen's throat buck nauseously every now and again. Yet he wanted to have a part in dressing it, and I was proud of him for that. He took up the game saw and cut off a shoulder and a ham. We had to lift the legs like pallbearers to get them to the boat. Blood ran from the meat and down my shirt with hideous, vital warmth.

The skiff sat low under the weight of our haul. The most substantial ballast of our crew, I sat in the stern and ran the kicker so the bow wouldn't swamp. Stephen sat on the cross bench, our knees nearly touching. We puttered out, a potent blue vapor bubbling up from the propeller. Clearing the shallows, I opened the throttle, and the craft bullied its way through the low swells, a fat white fluke churning up behind us. We skimmed out while the sun tipped west toward dark woods. The gridded rubber handle of the Evinrude thrummed in my palm. The wind dried the fluids on my cheeks and tossed Stephen's hair in a sparse frenzy. With the carcass receding behind us, it seemed I'd also escaped the blackness that had plagued me since Stephen's arrival. The return of George's expansiveness, the grueling ordeal of the butchery, the exhaustion in my limbs, the satisfaction in having made an unreasonably good shot that would feed my friend and me until the snow melted—it was glorious. I could feel absolution spread across the junk pit of my troubles as smoothly and securely as a motorized tarpaulin slides across a swimming pool.

And Stephen felt it, too, or something anyway. The old unarmored smile I knew from childhood brightened his haunted face, a tidy, compact bow of lip and tooth, alongside which I always looked dour and shabby in the family photographs. There's no point in trying to describe the love I can still feel for my brother when he looks at me this way, when he's stopped tallying his resentments against me and has briefly left off despising himself for failing to hit the big time as the next John Tesh. Ours isn't the kind of brotherhood I would wish on other men, but we are blessed with a single, simple gift: in these rare moments of happiness, we can share joy as passionately and single-mindedly as we do hatred. As we skimmed across the dimming lake, I could see how much it pleased him to see me at ease, to have his happiness magnified in my face and reflected back at him. No one said anything. This was love for us, or the best that love could do. I brought the boat in wide around the isthmus guarding the cove, letting the wake push us through the shallows to the launch where my sturdy blue truck was waiting.

With the truck loaded, and the skiff rinsed clean, we rode back to the mountain. It was past dinnertime when we reached my place. Our stomachs were yowling.

I asked George and Stephen if they wouldn't mind getting started butchering the meat while I put a few steaks on the grill. George said sure, but before he did any more work he was going to need to sit in a dry chair for a little while and drink two beers. He and Stephen sat and drank and I waded into the bed of my pickup, which was heaped nearly flush with meat. It was awful work rummaging in there, but I finally found the short ribs and I hacked out the tenderloin, a tapered log of flesh that looked like a peeled boa constrictor.

I held it up to show George.

He raised his can in tribute. "Now there's a pretty, pretty thing," he said.

I carried the loin to the porch and cut it into steaks two inches thick, which I patted with kosher salt and coarse pepper. I got the briquettes going while George and Stephen blocked out the meat on a plywood and sawhorse table in the headlights of my truck.

When the coals had grayed over, I dropped the steaks onto the grill. After ten minutes, they were still good and pink in the center, and I plated them with yellow rice. Then I opened up a bottle of burgundy I'd been saving and poured out three glasses. I was about to call the boys to the porch when I saw that something had caused George to pause in his labors. A grimace soured his features. He sniffed at his sleeve, then his knife, then the mound of meat in front of him. He winced, took a second careful whiff, and recoiled. "Oh, good Christ, it's turning," he said. With an urgent stride, he made for the truck and sprang onto the tailgate, taking up pieces of our kill and putting them to his face. "Son of a bitch," he said. "It's going off, all of it. Contaminated. It's something deep in the meat."

I walked over. I sniffed at the ham he'd been working on. It was true: there was a slight pungency to it, a diarrheal tang gathering in the air, but only faintly. If a bowel had leaked a little, it certainly wasn't any reason to toss thousands of dollars' worth of sustenance. And anyway, I had no idea how moose flesh was supposed to smell.

"It's just a little gamy," I said. "That's why they call it game."

Stephen smelled his hands. "George is right. It's spoiled. *Gah*."

"Not possible," I said. "This thing was breathing three hours ago. There's nothing wrong with it."

"It was sick," said George. "That thing was dying on its feet when you shot it."

"Bullshit," I said.

"Spoiled. I promise you," said George.

"No fucking way," I said. "It was fine when we broke it down."

George took a handkerchief from his pocket, spat on it, and scrubbed furiously at his palms. "Well it sure as hell ain't now. Took a little while to get going, I guess, but now it's gone, my friend. Goddammit, I should have known when the hide hung on there like it did. He was bloating up with something, just barely holding on. But the second he died, that infection turned loose and just started going wild."

Stephen looked at the flesh strewn across the table, and at the three of us standing there. Then he began to laugh.

I went to the porch and bent over a steaming steak. It smelled all right. I rubbed the salt crust and licked at the juice from my thumb. "There's nothing wrong with it," I said. I cut off a dripping pink cube and touched it to my tongue. Stephen was still laughing.

"You're a fucking star, Matty," he said, breathless. "All the beasts in the forest, and you mow down a leper. Don't touch that shit. Call in a hazmat team."

"There's nothing fucking wrong with this meat," I said.

"Poison," said George.

The wind gusted suddenly. A branch fell in the woods. A squad of leaves scuttled past my boots and settled against the door. Then the night went still again. I turned back to my plate and slipped the fork into my mouth.

EXECUTORS
OF
IMPORTANT
ENERGIES

The phone rang late, my stepmother again.

"Do you ever think about all the ones who you didn't let them have you? I wish I could take a do-over on all of them, even the nastiest. Even the worst. Are you there?"

"Yes," I said. "I'm just not sure what you want me to do with this information."

"Oh, forget it," she said. "I just don't feel very desirable is all."

I told her plenty of people desired her. "Well, nobody desires me to my face," she said.

"What time is it?"

"Not bad. Like three here. So it's two there. I figured you'd be up."

"I'm not up, Lucy. It's *four* here. Nobody's up right now."

"I am," she said. "And so is your dad. Down here, there's plenty of signs of life."

"I need to sleep," I said. "Go upstairs. Go to bed. I'll be in the shop tomorrow. Call me if you want."

"I'm staying right here," she said, and then came the smoggy burble of her water pipe. "It's pretty up-and-down with Roger. He's called the cops on me every night this week. So I just walk and walk until he goes to sleep. I've been walking so much, my ass is changing into a completely different thing."

"You should have told me," I said.

"I'm telling you now," she said. "Send you a picture if you like."

My father's troubles had started ten years or so ago when his memory started to erode. He lost wallets and sets of keys in increasingly quick succession. He lost his job, after repeatedly stranding his clients alone at the defense table while he wandered the streets, trying to recall which car was his. He'd more or less forgotten me two years ago, and then last month, he woke up from a two-day nap and couldn't recognize my stepmother. He called the police. She'd had to show two forms of ID not to get arrested for trespassing in her own house.

Nobody had a clear answer for what to do. We had looked into assisted-living places, but it was a ten-year waiting list if you weren't looking for a shrieking bedlam multiply indicted for filth and abuse. Other than putting up with my father, Lucy didn't work. She survived on his savings. My father was only sixty years old and otherwise in good health. He could go on absorbing cash and worry for another twenty-five years at least.

The sound of women screaming came in through my window. This was Thursday, and dance night at the lesbian bar up the block. Afterward, it was a regular thing for the women to stop by and use the west wall of my building to beat each other up against. They broke each other's hearts on schedule, always in the same indigo half hour of the morning. Sometimes, I'd look out the window and do them the favor of calling to them, so they could unite against me, a common enemy. But I cranked the pane shut and got back into bed.

"So look," Lucy was saying, "I'm thinking I'll bring him up there on the twentieth. The doctor said it might do him good to look at New York and to see you, too. Maybe jog some stuff loose for him."

I heard the scrabbling of rats' nails in the tin ceiling above my bed. "Please don't come, Lucy. I've got a thing to go to. And anyway, he doesn't even remember my name."

"Sure he does," she said. "He's been asking about you."

"That can't be true."

"It is. He was. Just yesterday. He drank a beer too fast, and then you should have heard him going, *Burrrt, Burrrt, Burrrt.*" She didn't laugh and neither did I.

"Please don't fucking bring him here," I said. "It's not a good idea."

"Be gentle," Lucy said, and got off the phone.

I was ten when my father married Lucy. He was forty-six. She was twenty-one, a secretary at his law firm, a job she'd planned to quit once her acting career took off. Her looks were good enough for it. She had the kind of hungry, large-eyed prettiness around which Japanese cartoonists have established whole religions of lechery. When I was young, before there was hair on my lip, I'd had a hard crush on her, and in some dim way, I was sure that my father was only with her temporarily, that he planned to turn her over to me someday. The particulars weren't absolutely clear, but I had a hunch that somewhere around my sixteenth birthday, he was going to take me out to a desert overlook where the sun was going down and announce that he was giving Lucy to me, along with his Mustang fastback, along with some Schlitz, and maybe a cassette tape that was nothing but "Night Moves" by Bob Seger and the Silver Bullet Band.

They had about three years of kindness with each other. Then Lucy met a man her age who wrote music for television commercials and went with him to Quebec. My father felt astonished in his grief—pushing fifty, the silver tufts bursting from his ears, to find his heart broken for the first time in his life. That was the one time he tried hard to be my friend. He had me over on weekends. He'd tell me love was like the chicken pox, a thing to get through early because it could really kill you in your later years. He'd bare his heart to me for an hour or two, and then he'd make me play chess with him, twenty, thirty games a weekend, and I'd lose every time.

Only once did I come close to beating him. He'd had some cocktails, and he blundered, moving his queen into the path of my knight. I sacked the piece, and he slapped me on the mouth. I ran into the bathroom and punched myself several times to ensure a lasting bruise. When I emerged, he didn't apologize, not exactly. But he said he'd give me anything I wanted not to tell my mother about it. I said I'd take a computer and a CO_2 BB gun. My father drew up a contract on his firm's letterhead, and I signed. We bought the gun that day. I used it to shoot a pretty lemon-colored warbler, which I stroked, then buried in my mother's lawn. Then I shot a dove and a chickadee, and gave the gun to the kid who lived next door.

After four months in Canada, Lucy came home. My father took her back without forgiving her, then went on to betray her many times, believing it was something he owed them both. He installed Lucy in an echoing faux-Tudor keep where all the sunlight in the place would not have been enough to run a solar calculator. Lucy grew depressed. She blamed her body, and punished it with starvation diets and triathlons. At the height of her regime, she was a new kind of creature, a lemur's head stuck to the body of a springbok. When a late bloom of acne speckled her cheeks, she convinced her therapist to write her a prescription for some drastic tablets, under threat of suicide. The pills took care of her seven pimples but crazed her face, chin to hairline, with little crimson fissures. She'd had to lather up with so many creams and unguents it looked like she was sweating lithium grease. Somewhere in there, I stopped dreaming of Lucy, the fastback, and the back rooms, the alleys and the trusty woods.

I was in my twenties when my father's mind began to go. At first, I thought his failure to remember where I was living, or that I'd finished school, was just a deepening of the aggressive indifference with which he'd always treated me, but it turned out to be something that a dozen good neurologists couldn't figure out. It wasn't Alzheimer's or any of the known dementias. His store of recollections just sprang a rapidly widening leak, starting with the short-term memories and then draining the older vaults. Within three years of the first symptoms, he couldn't recall what you'd told him an hour before. Couldn't work, couldn't find his own way home from the grocery store where he'd been shopping all his life. But he hadn't lost all capacity for deep, or at least medium, retrieval. My father was already forgetting my name when I mentioned to my mother, a few years back, the time he'd slapped me over the chessboard. Yet a few weeks after that, I received in the mail a copy of our old contract, along with a bill for $1,200—reimbursement for the computer and the BB gun, for which my father had kept receipts.

In college, I studied physics, engineering, and industrial design. I thought I would make airplanes, but after graduation I took a job drafting clock radio housings for the Emerson Corporation. Emerson put a great emphasis on anonymous roundness and dull curves, as though the idea was to slip our clocks unnoticed past the consumers' vision, like well-greased pills for your eye. After six years of that, I went out on my own. You could say I'd had one real success, a machine that melted down your spare plastic grocery bags and poured the rendered plastic into interchangeable molds (golf tee, pocket comb, bicycle tire lever, etc.). The device ranked high on a "Great Green Gifts" list in a major magazine, and since then the in-flight catalogs and shopping channels had picked it up. I wasn't getting rich off of it, but it was keeping me afloat. I had a studio apartment in the West Village, which people were impressed by until they came up for a look. The place was the architectural equivalent of a biscuit dough remnant, a two-hundred-square-foot waste shape of crannies and recesses left over when the rest of the building had been sectioned into proper places to live.

The day my father and Lucy were due to arrive, I'd booked myself a booth at the Service and Hospitality Expo in Westport, Connecticut. I went there to flog a device I was calling the Icepresto. It was basically a commercial coffee cistern with a copper heat-transfer coil in the base so you could brew a fresh pot of tea and pour it right away into a glass without melting your ice. I was hoping I could sell the patent for a hundred thousand or so and then hurry to the Gulf Coast to cram a pontoon boat and a big-titted stranger into the hollow places in my heart. But all day, I brewed and poured iced Earl Grey into Dixie cups for men in pleated slacks. They kept one hand in their pockets so I couldn't snap my card into their palms.

At the reception afterward, I tried to earn back my booth fee at the open bar. I went on the dance floor and got close to a young woman.

"Let's go have a look at the moon," I said.

"It's three o'clock," she said.

I walked back toward the train. The first hard snap of autumn was in the air. I felt the ache of it, rumbling toward the city with my cistern in my lap.

I got a message from Lucy telling me to meet them in Washington Square Park, where my father was watching chess. I rode the subway to Astor Place and walked west under a load of mounting dread. I hadn't seen him in fifteen months. I imagined him perched on a railing, with dusk coming on, craning at the Rollerbladers, drug merchants, and guitarists, like Rip Van Winkle come down from the hills, his hair a mess, a diaper smell coming off him, possibly.

But I found my father sitting at a table, looking fine, especially compared with his company, an obese chess hustler whose face was the gray-green hue of roofing slate. My father's hair was trimmed and combed in a tidy swale across his high forehead. He wore a clean white shirt and a crimson tie beneath an overcoat I'd never seen before: knee-length, clam-tone suede with a collar of black fur, a coat for the czar of the Wild West. I didn't go right to him. I stood ten feet away and watched him play. From that distance, you couldn't tell there was anything wrong with him, though his position was a losing one, his king on the back rank, pinned down by two bishops and a knight. Then my father threw up his hands and said something to the hustler. They laughed loud and long, like old friends, and I was glad. A love of strangers, a fearlessness with them, had always been one of my father's gifts. A connoisseur of the chance encounter, he would have tried to speak the language of cockatoos if one touched down beside him. He shook the man's hand, and they began setting up the pieces once more. I went to him before the game got under way. "Dad," I said, and wished in-

stantly that I'd let him be. The pleasure left his face, and his eyes
went vague with suspicion. He cowered slightly, seeming to recognize me not as son but as some unremembered person come
back from his past to pelt him with something.

"Dad, it's Burt," I told him.

He touched his finger to his ear. "Can't hear," he said.

"It's Burt," I said. "It's your son."

The news sent him into his familiar tic, a trembling reverse
yawn that seized him in moments of perplexity. The movement
of his jaw behind his closed lips lent an illusion that he lacked a
full set of teeth.

"Right, right, nice to see you," he said. He reached out and
brushed his fingers against my abdomen, as though to be sure I
wasn't a ghost. Then he cast a nervous eye at the hustler, as
though, above all things, my father didn't want to let the stranger
in on the secret of his deteriorating mind.

"Burt, Wade," my father said gruffly, gesturing at the large man,
who was scratching the thatch on his neck with a dirty nail.

"Dwayne," the man said. I shook his hand, which, despite
the cool weather, gave off a feverish warmth. He smiled. His
front tooth was broken at an angle, a tiny gray guillotine.

"Wade is a murderer on the chessboard," my father said. "A
lethal tactician. But you watch, Burt. I'll return from this slaughter and prevail."

"You're the shark here, Roger," said Dwayne. "I'm just a little
fish, trying to get a nibble where I can."

My father glared at the board. The black pieces were before
him. "Now hold on here, I'm white."

"Uh-uh, Rog. You were white last game. Don't think I forgot.
I got a mind like a steel trap."

"Have it your way." My father hit the clock.

Overhead, a large blue violence of storm clouds had begun to swell, but my father took no notice. He hunched to the game, giving me his broad sueded back.

I spotted my stepmother by the dry fountain, where she was watching some young people make a film. I left my cistern at my father's feet and jogged to her. Since I'd seen her last, Lucy had reached a new status of tiredness and age. Looking at her, "lady" is what I thought, a word that summed up her sparse, dry hair, her mottled cheeks, her many clattering bracelets and her lipstick, an alarming coral shade leaking into fresh hairline rills around her mouth. Her right eye was bloodshot and brimming with brine. We embraced. All she wore against the chill was a lamé shawl over a flimsy black top, so thin I could feel the gooseflesh on her hard arms.

"How long's he kept you out here?" I asked her.

"Three hours. I think him and that fat person are about ready to go off somewhere and have a civil union."

"We're going. I'll grab him."

"It's all right. I'm only cold on my body. He's happy. Let him play."

I pointed at her eye. "Are you high, Luce? Half high?"

"Big Iranian bitch on my volleyball team. Stuck her finger down my eye. Seeing double now."

I said I was sorry to hear it. She shrugged. "Beer helps," she said.

Lucy's gaze drifted back to the little film crew doing their shoot. The movie revolved around a single special effect: a narrow youth with a vest of birdseed glued to his nude chest to provoke a pigeon attack. Cameras were poised but the pigeons were not cooperating. Too much free seed was falling off of him, and so no birds were bothering to peck him on the skin.

A girl in ratty hair and paint-speckled jeans walked over. She'd written "Producer" in Magic Marker on her shirt. "You're in our shot. Would you mind getting out of the way?" the girl said, looking at Lucy as though offended by her makeup and glinting shawl.

"Yeah, kind of," Lucy said.

"Excuse me?" the girl said.

She and the girl might have had words had not my father's shouting voice come to us from the chess tables, so loud and urgent I thought he'd been attacked.

We ran to him, but there was no emergency. He'd won a game was all. He was still in a gloater's ecstasy when we reached him. "Oh, God, yes," he was saying. "Oh, man alive, does that feel good."

"You sure put me in trouble, Roger," Dwayne said. "One more, now? For tens?"

But my father wasn't ready to leave aside the glory of the moment. "To hell with orgasms," he mused, leaning into the table. "I'll take a clean rook-ending any day. I mean, Jesus, Wade, what is it? What is it that makes it such a joy to beat a man at chess?"

"Music," the hustler said. "Artistry and shit. Now, tens?"

The storm wind rose, and my father cocked his head to watch a flock of sycamore leaves swirling down. His fur collar stirred against his jaw.

"You like this coat?" Lucy asked me. "He saw it in the window at Barney's. Eighteen hundred bucks."

My father glanced at us with a halfway scowl and turned back Dwayne.

"Fischer said, 'Chess is life,'" announced my father.

Dwayne ran his tongue under his lip. "Fischer said all sorts of stuff," he replied. "He said there were tiny Jews living in his teeth."

"It's *better* than life. In the world, there's no such thing as a clean escape, if you follow me," my father said. "I mean, you could keep cleaning my clock all night, but at the end of the day, you've still got a broken tooth and a snot booger on your collar and a head full of garbage that keeps you up at night, but—"

"Hey, motherfucker, be nice," said Dwayne.

The rain began, a soft silver sound in the high dry leaves. The loose crowd of spectators dispersed. The other hustlers turned peevish faces toward the sky, then rolled up their boards and folded them into long zippered cases.

"Italian," my father said. "That's what I could go for now."

"We do have a tab, here, Roger," said Dwayne.

My father's losses came to forty dollars, but Dwayne did not look pleased, even as he pocketed the bills. Dwayne held out his hand to the rain, and the drops made dark spots on his dry hand. He shook his head. "Rain is a heavenly thing," he said. "And it comes to us from a heavenly direction, but it does make for one unheavenly motherfucker of an evening out here on this boulevard."

My father turned to Dwayne and fixed him with a stern, paternal look.

"You look like a veal man to me," my father said. "When's the last time somebody set you up with a nice hot plate of veal?"

"I can't recall," said Dwayne.

"You come with me," my father said. "We'll get you squared away."

"Roger—" Lucy started.

"Uh-oh," said my father gravely. He was staring down at his right shoe. The laces had come undone, and he squinted up at Lucy and me, uncertain and overwhelmed by this new problem whose scope he seemed unable to gauge. Without hesitating, Lucy knelt and tied his shoe. Then she set off toward MacDougal Street. "There's a jolly person," said my father, watching Lucy's rump swinging in her jeans. "Does she go to your school?"

The restaurant Lucy chose was an old-style place of dark wood where large men in collared shirts stood at the bar and roared at one another over a calming frenzy of piped-in mandolins.

"Does this look all right to you, Rog?" Lucy asked my father.

My father turned to Dwayne and clapped a hand to his meaty upper arm. "What say, there, Wade? How's your appetite, buddy? Ready to hit a lick on some veal?"

"Let it happen," said Dwayne.

The host appraised us—Dwayne, my father in his haute Western upholstery, Lucy and her weeping eye—and led us to a dark rear room. The only other diners there were a well-dressed elderly black couple who had the enclosed, penitent air of people who had just finished an argument.

"Piña colada, please," Dwayne told the host before we sat.

"Your server will be here in just a moment," he said.

"Piña colada! Make it two. One for him, one for me," my father said.

"Beer," said Lucy. "Whatever's coldest. Vodka back."

The host departed in a smolder. My father looked down at my tea cistern, which stood between our chairs.

"What the hell is that thing?" he asked.

I explained it to him.

"You're in the beverage trade?" he asked.

"I'm an industrial designer. An inventor. You know that, Dad."

He grunted. "Go to law school. Make a difference."

"I do make a difference," I said. He looked at me. I sputtered on about what a grand business it was, to be a foot soldier in mankind's never-ending struggle for convenience, and how the small, unobserved technologies—remote key fobs, ballpoint pens, Q-tips—shaped our lives in more significant ways than music, books, or film. "People who do what I do, Dad, we're the executors of important energies, the same stuff that builds nations, the conviction that—"

The waiter arrived, and my father lunged for his piña colada. Then he sucked at it as though it were an oxygen mask.

"You have to help me here," said Lucy quietly.

"With what?" I asked.

"Don't let him get a second drink," she said. "It's the meds, I guess. He can't handle it anymore. He had three wines at the Angus Barn a few weeks back. He was eating stew with his hands. Ow, fuck."

Lucy reached a hand under her shirt to attend to a stiff thread poking her ribs. Dwayne watched her with a goatish look.

"Can I help you?" Lucy asked him.

"Undoubtedly," he said. "You're helping me right now."

Lucy looked to my father, who had turned sideways in his chair, watching the black couple's table, where the waiter was demonstrating a bottle of white wine.

"Look at that," he said. "We got here first, and they're being served already."

"No," I said. "*They* got here first. *We've* been served already."

But he seemed not to hear. The spectacle of the waiter pouring a tasting portion into our neighbor's glass captivated him. The man sipped and gave a curt nod. "Look, they poured out the wine for that black man to taste," my father said, leering in wonderment at the man's precocity, as though he were watching a squirrel wash a cracker. "Isn't that something?"

This stunned me. My father had been in many ways a rough, unpleasant man, though dislike of one race or another had never been one of his pet brutalities. During his legal career, he'd prided himself on being a fierce egalitarian and a stalwart for unpopular causes, though it seemed to me he tussled less for righteousness than the pleasure of the fight. In his pro bono work, he liked representing doers of sensational evil and generally got good results for them in court. Dungeon keepers. Home invaders with a taste for elder flesh. A boy, now famous in death for his botched ride in the electric chair, who killed a woman with a brake shoe and left her infant crawling the shoulder of a rural route. He found much pleasure in recounting for my mother and me the stories of his "guys," the details of their cases, the last expressions of the murdered, etc., to confirm himself as the captain of all knowledge, ugly and good. Before I'd finished second grade, my father was imparting axioms like "Burt, fight to the death before you let somebody put you in his car. Either way, you're probably dead, and believe me, it's better to check out before they get creative on you."

But he also went after quieter cases, too: housing and hiring discrimination, worker's compensation. Though I'd always sensed something cheap and spiteful in my father's righteousness — an easy way for him to put himself above the rest of us — he did win a lot of money for people who needed it. It's probably true that my father did more good for other people in his work than I ever will in my career. The merry bigot before me now depressed me as deeply as anything I'd seen in his decline.

Back at the couple's table, the asperity I'd noticed when we first walked in seemed to have recongealed. "It wasn't Villainy, Judith," the man snapped at his companion. "It was *Villandry*. That was the place we rode the bikes along the river and the hotel leaked and you ate that pork loin cooked in pâté and you got a stomachache. *Villandry*. Whoever heard of a town called Villainy?"

My father shook his head, frowning in mock-rueful satisfaction. "They can dress up, can't they?" he said. "But they still act the same."

Then he stood, and I was afraid he was going to go to the couple's table and bait them in some way, but he made for the restroom.

"Is he okay in there by himself?" I asked Lucy.

"He can still recognize a toilet, thank God."

Dwayne took a roll from the bread basket, tore it in half, and pressed it flat into the olive oil dish. He had his eyes on Lucy while he chewed.

"I know a man you need to meet," he said.

"Oh, good," said Lucy.

"You ever hear of Aristedes Fontenot?" Dwayne said. "Top sculptor in New York. Friend of mine. I know he will want to make a statue of your face."

Lucy took a breath to say something, but instead she hailed the waiter for another vodka.

"He's your husband," Dwayne said, jerking his head toward the bathroom.

"Yeah," said Lucy.

"He doesn't act like it," Dwayne said.

"I don't see how that's your business," Lucy said.

"Just let me say this," Dwayne said with a cockeyed grin. "If I had someone nice-looking like you, I'd act like it till there wasn't none left."

Lucy closed her eyes and laughed and Dwayne laughed, too. "I like you, Dwayne," she said. "Come on, let's go out back." She smacked the table with her hand. "You think they got an 'out back' at this joint?"

"Lucy, please stop," I said. My father had emerged from the restroom and was walking toward us.

She covered half her face with her hand and looked at Dwayne with her injured eye. "Why?" she said. "He looks pretty good like this."

"Talk to me, Dwayne," said Lucy, when all the bread had been eaten and the conversation flagged and the feeling at the table was of strangers on a cruise, seated together by happenstance. "You make your living that way? Hustling chess in the park?"

"I suppose, if you can call it a living."

"What do you call it, Dwayne?" she asked him.

"Well, the game is a lucrative addiction. In my soul, I am a musician."

I asked Dwayne what he played, and before he could answer, my father sat forward in his seat and began to clear his throat at full volume, an angry, engine-revving sound. "So, Wade," my father said gruffly.

"Yes, Roger?"

My father didn't answer. His lips moved silently, and I realized he had nothing to say. He only wished to keep Lucy and me from getting a word in with Dwayne, whom he apparently considered a special friend he didn't want to share. My father's long-standing fondness for strangers aside, it baffled me that he'd taken such a passionate liking to the hustler. But then, perhaps it was this: perhaps he knew he was slipping away from Lucy and me. He felt the terrible humiliation of it, and could be at ease only in the company of someone with whom he had no past to forget.

We watched my father, his mouth opening and closing, his shoulders hunched, his eyes cast down.

"Paul Morphy," he said at last. "Opera Game. Black takes the Philidor Defense, am I right?"

"My friend, I could not say," said Dwayne.

My father pursed his lips, dismayed. "Waiter," he called out, rattling the ice in his glass. "Drought conditions over here."

"How about let's hold off there, Pops," I said.

"How about you kiss my ass?"

"In answer to your question, Burt, I am a horn player," Dwayne said, miming a flurry of saxophone riffs. The fingerings looked fairly professional. "I sing as well. Are you familiar with the recording artist Kenny Loggins?"

"You played with Kenny Loggins?" Lucy said.

"I did blow for Kenny on the European tour. My wife and me, we also blessed his outfit with some very beautiful backing vocals. Saw all the top destinations, stayed in fine hotels, rode all the major airlines, Qantas, Virgin Atlantic. I'm glad you brought it up. That was a happy time of life."

"You still married, Dwayne?" she asked.

"Enough about me," Dwayne said. "I'm getting depressed."

"You used to sing, Roger," said Lucy. "I'd forgotten that about you."

"I did?" my father said.

"Yeah, you did," said Lucy. "Mornings. You sang a lot in the mornings."

My father grasped the saltshaker with both hands and ran his thumbnail pensively along the grid of rumpled glass. "What'd I sing?" he asked without looking up.

"Sam Cooke. Elvis. Some Leonard Cohen. You did a pretty good Velvet Fog."

He looked at her, and I could see the muscles around his eyes tense for a moment and then relax. "You've got your facts screwed up."

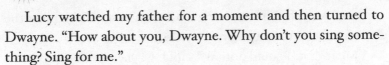

Lucy watched my father for a moment and then turned to Dwayne. "How about you, Dwayne. Why don't you sing something? Sing for me."

"Right here?"

"Yes," said Lucy. "Sing for me right here."

So Dwayne started to hum a little overture, and even that hum was a thing of real quality, a practiced, dusky baritone, and he knew how to make it swell from the deep place in his chest. The couple at the next table looked over at him, ready to get mad, but they held off, looking unsure of themselves, wondering perhaps if Dwayne might be a famous man caught in a late-career spell of bad luck. Then the singing started, some old song I'd never heard before. Whatever it was, Dwayne sang it in a wondrous way. The melody unraveled in a barreling curve that only hovered near the song's true line, corkscrewing up out of the tune. He sang in many voices at once, a roisterous calliope. At the front, a slick, showy tenor; behind that, a lumbering, tuneful goon chiming in on the bass; and a manic soprano wandering in and out of the line.

Lucy's pleasure in the moment was wonderful to see. She let her head loll on her shoulder, showing the handsome vein in her neck. Her face went young with joy and shyness. Sand filled my thoat, and I saw my father's wife as I'd wanted her many years ago.

Only my father didn't share in the gladness of the room. He stretched his jaw in the usual tic. He gripped his butter knife hard enough to pale his knuckles, and I was afraid he was going to smash his plate with it. But then Dwayne wound to his final flourish. Lucy led the applause. Dwayne's small reptilian eyes swiveled in his head. "Usually, for that type of performance, five dollars is the standard contribution."

Lucy laughed. "I'll give you five bucks, but first you have to sing me one more song."

Dwayne shrugged. "You're fucking with a man's price structure, but all right. Let's see."

"No more," my father barked. He was scanning the tablecloth irritably, as though something he'd misplaced was there, hiding in plain sight. "No more songs. This is a restaurant, for Christ's sake, and speaking of, can somebody tell me where the hell is that veal?"

"Just shut up," Lucy told my father. "Would you please shut up, Roger? Just this one time?"

My father's nostrils flared, and his features distended in sneering contempt. Cupping a hand to his mouth, he turned to Dwayne. "Now, I don't know who this woman is," he said in a voice loud enough for the room to hear, "and I don't know why she's in my house with me. But I'll be honest with you. I think I'd like to try and fuck her."

Dwayne burst into braying laughter, and so did the barroom men and so did the boy in the clip-on tie lingering in the door. Lucy's face was blank. With perfect calmness, she reached across the table and took a cigarette from the pack of Newports at Dwayne's elbow. We all watched her stand and yank the coat from the back of my father's chair. He pitched forward slightly. His fork hit the bell of his empty wineglass, striking a high, clean note that went on ringing until his wife was out the door.

I bolted down my gnocchi so quickly that it formed a baseball in my throat, while my father and Dwayne sucked and panted over their scaloppine. I was rigid with anger, at the farce of the dinner, at having wasted an evening that at this time tomorrow my father surely wouldn't recall. As soon as Lucy returned to the beef cheeks congealing on her plate, I planned to excuse myself and go home.

But ten, fifteen, twenty minutes passed and Lucy didn't reappear. I rose. I couldn't find her in the bar, and she wasn't out smoking on the sidewalk. The uncivil waitress I enlisted couldn't find her in the ladies' room.

"She's gone, incidentally," I told my father.

He frowned and grunted, as though I'd just read him a distressing headline on a subject he didn't entirely understand. I tried Lucy's phone. It rang in my father's pants.

We loitered for another twenty minutes over coffee. By then the place was filling up and the waiter, unbidden, delivered our check. My father gazed down at the little folio but didn't open it. His eyes were tired and dull with colada rheum. "A hundred and fifty-seven bucks, Dad," I said, reading the bill. "Thank you, by the way."

"I can't pay," my father said.

"Why not?"

"Wallet's in my coat," my father said. I sighed and slipped my credit card into the plastic flap.

Out on the sidewalk, rain had stopped, but the autumn chill had solidified into a true and bitter cold. My father, in his shirt-sleeves, wrapped his arms about himself and shrank into his collar. "I'm putting you in a cab," I said. "What's your hotel?"

"Not sure," he said.

"Son of a bitch," I cried. "You don't know?" I grabbed my father and turned his pockets out, looking for a room key or a card. He submitted to the search without protest, looking at me with fearful eyes.

"That's cold," clucked Dwayne, who for reasons that weren't

clear had not yet bid us adieu. "Shaking your old man down like that."

"Stay out of it," I snapped. "We've got to find her. She's walking. I guess I'll just spend a fucking fortune on a cab and see if we can find her on the street."

"If I may," said Dwayne, "I do have a vehicle at my disposal. It would be my pleasure to drive you boys around."

"You've got a car, Dwayne?" I said.

"I do indeed," he said. "Just around the corner. I'll go get it. One small difficulty. Where I have it stowed, I need a dub to get it out."

"What's he want?" my father asked.

"He wants twenty dollars," I said.

"Okay. So give it to him."

"I don't think I will."

"Quit dicking around," my father said. "It's late and I'm tired. Give him that money."

I gave Dwayne the bill, and he sauntered off down the street. My father clutched himself while the traffic bleated and the crowds brushed past and the wind made a frowsy ruin of his thin gray hair. "It sure will be nice to get into that car," he said.

"There isn't any car," I said. "He isn't coming back. That was another twenty dollars of mine you just threw away."

My father rocked back and forth on the soles of his feet and looked off in the direction Dwayne had gone.

"Tell me you're sorry," I told him.

He squinted against the wind, his face like a fist. "For what? For the money? For the bill?"

"Sure," I said. "Let's start there. The twenty. Say you're sorry for that."

He gazed down the sidewalk, where a pigeon was pecking

at a cocktail sword. It got the blade in its beak and waddled proudly down the street and vanished, turning right on Minetta Lane. At last, my father sighed and said something in a quiet, remorseful voice.

"What?" I said. "Say that again, so I can hear."

He grimaced, hunching slightly as though a sudden pain had gripped his stomach. "Bishop," he said, and turned away.

"Bishop," I repeated.

"Bishop to G-5 pins Black's knight against the queen."

Seconds later, an aged white Mercedes pulled up, Dwayne's wide greenish face leering at us from behind the wheel. Dwayne reached over and let the passenger door swing wide. "You came back," I said.

"True," said Dwayne.

The backseat was full of newspapers and bedding. A grim reek of urine and old laundry was close in the car. My father and I shouldered in together on the bench seat. Wind was blowing through the passenger's-side window, and when I reached across my father to work the crank, a crumbling horizon of glass rose in the pane and spilled into my father's lap.

"Yeah. Some asshole broke that out," said Dwayne.

My father said nothing. His teeth were chattering, and his lips hung slack and wet. He looked hopelessly old, and his eyes were large and vacant. A sorrow hit me then, and I might have embraced him or taken his hand, but Dwayne hit the gas, and the Mercedes leaped across Houston Street. We struck a pothole with a heavy thud. The impact sent swaying the load of junk and bangles hanging from Dwayne's rearview—Mardi Gras beads, feathered gewgaws, sports medallions—and my father watched the swinging mess with all the fascination of an infant watching the mobile over his crib. He reached out and caught hold of a miniature New Mexico license plate. He frowned at the embossed letters reading "Land of Enchantment."

"What is this?" he asked.

"It's just some bullshit I picked up on the road," said Dwayne.

"No, this word here, 'enchantment.' What's that mean, again?"

"Shit," said Dwayne. "You know what charm is, Roger?"

"Of course," my father said.

"It's like that, like charm."

My father leaned against me, studying the orange Braille. "Land of Charm," he said.

DOWN
THROUGH
THE
VALLEY

When Jane left me for Barry Kramer, it was a heavy kind of hurt, but by the time she took up with him, there wasn't a whole lot left of us. For quite a while, we'd been nothing but an argument looking for different ways to happen. Barry had been her meditation instructor, something he did before he started his business of going around to companies and teaching managers how to keep the lines of communication open. I had ignored the advice of friends and encouraged her relationship with Barry because her sessions with him did seem to calm Jane somewhat and also made her less inclined to drink herself into black dudgeon and curse me for the years she couldn't get back. But it was not a pleasant surprise when I came home one afternoon, and there, in the sunlight on our living room floor, was Jane sitting in her brassiere, Barry's hands on her bare shoulders. When I walked in with our daughter, Marie, they both jumped up and started laying on about how Barry was just showing off some new shiatsu moves. I then lashed out at Barry with a piece of hose I'd brought home to stick on the bath spigot. I shouted and made my daughter cry. I broke some things. I made promises of more and worse violence, and Jane left with Barry and Marie. I remember her standing in the doorway with an armful of clothes, her jaw muscles standing out and her telling me how I'd rue what I had done.

And she was right: I did wind up ruing it, but after a while, neither often nor deeply. Jane bought out my share of our house at a fair price. I took a place outside of town, a redone shotgun cottage on six acres with a creek running through the yard. The house suited me well, except for a million black wasps chewing holes in the clapboards. The little fellows made an awful grinding racket, and on weekend afternoons when feelings of failure and regret could not be kept at bay, I found pleasant distraction in squirting poison up those holes.

I dug myself a garden, and a stray cat I grew to like would come around to sulk in the corn. I forced myself to seek new love, and for a while, I thought I'd found it with a girl from my office. She was molten in my bed, but she also suffered depressions that were very dear to her. She would often call just to sigh at me for two hours on the phone, wanting me to applaud her depth of feeling. I cut it off, then missed her, wishing that I'd at least had the sense to take her naked photograph.

I saw Jane once each month, the day I came by to borrow Marie. Jane was prettier now that she'd given up alcohol for the herbal program Barry'd put her on. She didn't seem to hate me anymore, and usually received me with a kind of sour concern. "I was sorry to see you sneaking past the house the other night," she said one time. "It's not good for you. Also, if you're going to make spying on people a regular thing, you should fix your exhaust. Sounds like someone in a suit of armor getting dragged up the street."

Mercifully, she was gone most of the summer after our separation, to Mendocino, California, Barry's hometown, to Oregon and Sedona, Arizona, and then back here and off again soon after to a retreat up in the mountains to interface with cedar trees and experience cosmic episodes. Jane surprised me with a phone call early one morning in September. I was awake already, listening to the wasps eat my house.

"We had an accident up here at the ashram," Jane said. "I need you to come get Marie—Barry, too, if it's all right."

I got hot with her, thinking that Marie had hurt herself while the grown-ups were off grooving on the nectar of supreme instruction, but Jane said no, it was Barry. He had fallen off the roof or something, and now he needed to come home because he couldn't do any postures on a busted ankle. She explained that Barry was not in a way to operate a clutch pedal or to pitch in on babysitting while Jane was on a session. It would really help, she said, if I would come and do this thing.

I didn't like driving my car too far past the city limits, and I wasn't overly excited by the notion of a long ride with Barry Kramer. But I was heartened that Jane wanted to get us to a place where we could start doing favors for each other. It was her sort of olive branch, more wood than fruit. I told her okay.

The retreat was up in the western part of the state, three hours away. I followed Jane's directions down some winding back roads, parked and got out in a very nice spot, a wide field of goldenrod running down to a lake the color of new blue jeans, with thick black woods darkening the water's edge. Not long ago, I'd read in the papers about a woman who died near here under strange circumstances. She'd disappeared one weekend, camping with her husband. The papers painted it like he'd killed her, but just before the police booked him, a hunter had shot a black bear with part of the lady's hat in its stomach, a funny kind of good news for the widower.

Walking down to the compound, I passed a young woman sitting on a picnic table with a baby at her breast. Little kids were doing the bat-hang on a wooden jungle gym. A boy who was hoeing up a pea patch said he knew my ex-wife and pointed at the canvas hut where she was staying.

Barry was sitting on the floor in there with his bad foot up on a bench. He watched me come in. His beard had more white hairs in it than when I'd seen him last, but he was still a handsome man. No belly, smooth skin, full head of hair, better-looking than me. "Hi there, Ed," he said. Jane hadn't been kidding about that foot. It was in awful shape: gray from toe to shin with a swirling purple galaxy of a bruise over his anklebone.

I went and shook his hand. "Damn, Barry," I said. "You should've called me up before gangrene set in."

He looked at his foot and made a gesture like he was waving away a smell. "Bad sprain, that's all. Nothing to it. Just need to give it some R & R and let the body do the rest. The pisser is I put down a deposit to stay through the first, and they won't give it back. You might think it's share and share alike in a place like this, but believe me, these people count every bean."

The door slammed and Marie came in. When she saw me, she closed one eye and shied away in put-on bashfulness. Then she held out her arms for me to snatch her up, which I did.

"I was playing with Justin and look what I got," she said, angling her wrist at my face. The skin there was raw and sticky. "Poison sumac," she said with pride.

"Yuck," I said. I set her down again. "Hey, Barry, I might like to say hi to Jane, if you know where she's at." I hadn't told her yet I'd filed papers at work for a move to Hot Springs, where a new branch was opening up. I'd get a raise if the job came through, and I'd have some people working under me. I wanted to catch her up on that.

Barry shook his head. "Can't happen, I'm sorry," he said. "She's in the middle of an isolation."

"Well, I'll just stick my head in and say hey real quick."

"I'm sorry, but they won't let her have visitors right now, not me or anybody. Not for thirty-six hours. Maybe you'd like to leave a note."

I thought about it. "Nah, don't guess I need to. Might as well just hit the road."

Barry pulled himself up on an old metal crutch with a folded towel where the pad was missing. I tried to take his pack for him, but he made a show of wanting to carry it himself. He struggled behind me up the path, having to stop about every five steps to hitch the strap.

We reached the car, and I held the door open for him, but he didn't climb in right away. He stood there rocking on his crutch, gazing off at the sky and the fields and the fall trees starting to go the color of sherbet. He scratched his sooty beard and took in loud, greedy breaths. "Man, will I miss this," he said. "Actual, clean air. Thank God there's something left the bastards haven't been able to slap a brand name on yet. Kills me to leave this place."

A flock of geese rose from the far side of the lake and drifted into a spotty boomerang formation overhead. Barry hoisted Marie up so she could see over the car. One arm slid across her shoulders, the other caught her in the crook of her knees, and he propped my daughter on his stomach in a way that showed he'd held her like this many times before. With her eyes on the geese, Marie tugged idly on Barry's ear with her scabby little hand. I watched them, and they watched the geese, which called to each other in voices like nails being pulled from old boards.

I put the front seat up so Barry could crawl into the back and stretch out. He stuck his crutch in first and braced it on the seat as he eased himself into the car. The crutch didn't have a rubber stopper on the tip, and it hung up on the upholstery and ripped a little crown-shaped hole in the vinyl. Barry looked at me to see if I'd seen it, then gave a guilty wince.

"Ah, jeez," he said. "Barry, you clumsy son of a bitch."

I let out a breath. "No big thing," I told him.

He fingered the tear. "Tell you what. We'll get one of those kits. You know those things they sell? We can fix this, easy."

"Not a hole that big you can't. Forget it."

I moved to put the seat back, but Barry put his arm against it. "Hey, hey, hold on a second, Ed."

"What?"

"You don't need to get short with me. We'll fix it. If we can't do it ourselves, take it to a place, on me. Really."

"Nobody's getting short," I told him. "This car's a bucket. I could buy another one for what it'd cost to fix that rip. Now watch your arm."

"Can I give you a few bucks at least?" He reached for his wallet.

"No."

I strapped Marie into the shotgun seat, and we rode out of there. Soon we were rolling along the ridge that runs parallel to the state line.

Up ahead, looming over the road was a split crag of rock reaching high into the air. It had the look of a crow's head, its beak parted for the worm. "Hey, Marie, what's that rock look like to you?"

She thought it over. "An ass-butt," she said, and laughed like hell.

"Interesting," I said. "I don't see it."

"You know what that is?" Barry chimed in from the back. "That's actually the hardened lava from a dormant volcano. The outer layers of sediment weather much faster, so it just leaves you with a sort of a cast of the core of the mountain."

Soon Barry dozed off. He was leaning his head on the window just behind my seat, and his breath whistled through his thick mustache. There was a smell to him, soap and sweat and sour milk.

I asked a lot of people about Barry when Jane got mixed up with him. I knew a lady who'd legged down with him one time. She said the weird stink of him had been a problem, which I was pleased to hear. She also said that he had a huge banana, that he did breathing exercises beforehand, and that afterwards he'd gone in the kitchen and whipped up a big beet salad.

I looked in the rearview. Barry had his good foot propped on the back of Marie's seat. His pants were hiked up, showing a shin about as big around as a deer's leg, and covered so thickly in coarse black hair you could have hung a toothpick in it.

Already, I was regretting doing Jane this favor. My mind was wandering. You can't sit in a little Datsun car with your wife's new lover without recollecting all the nice old junk about her that you'd do better not to haul up. Her belly slumping against the small of your back on a cold morning. The slippery marvel of her soaped up in the shower. A night long ago when you moved on each other so sincerely that you sheared off two quarter-inch lag bolts that held your bed together. But start playing back all the old footage, and pretty soon Mendocino Barry steals into the frame, his bare dark-brindled haunches in your bed, candles and an incense stencher fuming on the nightstand. You can see him tucking a yellow thumbnail under the scalloped elastic of her bikini underpants and shucking them down slow, maybe with a word or two about lotus blossoms. You don't want to picture how she lifts her hips up off the bed, the openmouthed anticipatory shivers, or Barry rearing up in a sun salute between her splayed knees, his tongue lolling like a tiki god in ugly throes. You don't want to get into thoughts about Hovering Butterflies or the Jade Stalk, or the Door of the Holy Abode, when you can remember one time, a few times actually, when you came home late under a fair amount of liquor and you got on top of your sleeping wife, going, "Come on, Mother, can't we poon?"

It made me feel queasy. I shook off a shiver and I reached over and patted Marie on the head. She was starting to doze.

She wriggled under my hand. "Don't mess with me when I'm drowsy," she said.

We turned onto the skinny state highway that ran back down through the valley. To the west, the land plunged away, and down where the mountains flattened out, the green grid of farmlands looked crisp and vivid as a billiard table.

We rode for a while, and nobody talked. Marie played with her fingers and mumbled to herself. Outside, the sun was falling fast, letting big shadows pool up in the spaces between the hills. The other cars had their lights on now, and I clicked the knob for the headlamps and got the heat going, too. Marie stuck her hand in front of the vent to feel the hot air on her.

Heat was something me and Jane had liked to fight about. She could never get warm in our house. It could be the middle of July, and she'd want to shut the windows and put the furnace on. I wouldn't turn the thermostat past sixty-five, so she'd crank up the burners on the stove and hunch there, scowling, like a cavewoman guarding a coal. Often, the first thing I saw when I came home from work was Jane standing by the stove with her hair full of knots and an old T-shirt sagging close to the cooktop. I yelled at her about it, but that didn't help. Her nightgown went up in flames two times, and we had to stop, drop, and roll her on the kitchen floor.

The vinyl groaned behind me, and I heard Barry sit up and yawn.

"Hey, Barry, does Jane still do that thing where she tries to catch herself on fire with the stove?"

"Not that I've noticed," he said. I told him about her two accidents.

"Doesn't surprise me. She's got miserable circulation."

"Hey, does she still do that thing of leaving a bunch of snot rags all balled up in the bed? Man, I remember, she'd have so much old Kleenex going, you'd get in bed, and *crrrunch!* Make you want to puke. She still do that?"

Barry gave a dry laugh. "No comment," he said.

"Do what?"

"I'm sorry," Barry said. "This makes me a little uncomfortable, to be honest with you. Not fair to convict her without her here to defend herself."

"Just making conversation," I said. I let it go without asking him what I'd really wanted to know, which was whether Jane was still suffering this dream she kept having while we were married. Ever since she was a little girl, she'd had these two-ply nightmares where she dreamed that a man was standing over the bed. Then she'd dream that she'd woken up from the nightmare only to see that there really was a man standing over the bed. At that point, all hell would break loose. Sometimes, she'd jump out of bed and just start running. She hurt herself that way. She'd run into walls. Once, she tore through a sliding screen door. Sometimes the sheets would get tangled around her ankles and before she could even get going, she'd fall hard on her face, and by morning, she'd have a black eye coming into focus. Those dreams had always scared the hell out of me. Jane swore they didn't mean anything, that it wasn't what it looked like, a memory of somebody who'd been having her when she was a kid. I wanted to ask Barry if she'd brought up the nightmares in all that consciousness work they'd done together, but I had a feeling he'd have a way of turning it on me and making the dreams my fault.

The sky was going dark when Marie bent over in her seat and did a strange thing. She leaned her head down and put her lips on the gearshift. She got the whole thing in her mouth and it stretched her jaw open all the way. A ribbon of slobber slid down onto the gear boot and twinkled in the green glow of the dashboard. I waited for her to quit, but she didn't. She seemed to have fallen asleep like that. I tapped her on the back. "Okay, honey, quit it," I said. Barry's head was up in the rearview again, though his face was dark against the lights of the car behind us.

"It's all right, Ed," Barry said. "Jane and I let her do that on long trips. The vibrations relax her. She says it feels good on her teeth."

"Yeah, well, it's not safe," I said. "Come on, sweets, get off of there." I pulled on Marie's shoulder, but she wouldn't give up the shifter, didn't even stir. Some kids, you could put them in a barrel and roll them down a flight of stairs and they still wouldn't wake up. Marie's like that. "Marie, honey."

Barry made like he was going to say something, and then he didn't, and then he did. "Ed, if I may, I think you might just let her stay there. Jane says it's fine. There's no harm in it, really."

I looked at Marie down there with the gear knob buzzing away in her mouth. A spooky gagging hum was leaking out of her. It was really giving me the Larries. I put my hand under

Marie's jaw and pried her off of the shifter. The thing was, her teeth pinched up a little bit of her lip, and when she sat up in the seat, she blinked a few times, touched the little spot of blood in the corner of her mouth, and started to cry.

"Yeah, see, Ed, what I was trying to tell you is if you'd just let her—"

"Barry," I said. "Thanks for putting your spoke in, but I'd appreciate it if whatever you're going to say, you'd just shut up with it."

"Hey, come on, Ed, you don't have to get hostile with me here," he said.

Marie was taking in a long jagged breath that I knew was going to turn loud when it came back out.

"I'm not being hostile, Barry. I just don't need to hear from a goddamn committee right now."

Marie went into a long, low wail with a lot of lung power behind it. She did a couple of those, and then she just sat there and whined.

Barry let a second pass and then he said, "Is she hurt?"

"No, goddammit, Barry, she's not hurt." I rubbed Marie on her back. "Baby doll, you're okay, right?"

She huffed and sputtered and shook her head no.

"Oh, Jesus, yes you are, baby. You're just fine. Barry, she's fine. She's just got a little nick on her lip is all."

"She's bleeding?"

"Barry, will you please shut up for right now? Okay, please?" I turned to Marie and wiped a tear from her cheek. "Now, honey, how can I dry you up? You hungry? You want a milkshake? You want a goody?"

"No," she said, in about sixteen syllables.

"Oh, goddammit, yes you do," I said. I was in a mood to break something. I turned on the radio loud and punched the middle of the steering wheel, but gently, so as not to honk the horn.

A fog had followed us down from the mountains. Fence posts flickered quick and dim in the low beams. Cresting a hill, we surprised a possum eating something in the road. It wheeled around, its eyes glowing flat and yellow in the headlights.

Barry shifted, and again his head was up between the seats. "Ed, would you mind turning that down for a sec?"

I did.

"Sorry. I feel like I should say something," he said.

"That's all right. You said some things already."

"No, I want to apologize. It wasn't right for me to second-guess you back there. Part of me has a way of speaking up when it shouldn't."

"Forget it," I said.

Barry coughed into his hand. "Hey, Ed, look, I want you to know, I really appreciate this favor of you coming out and giving me a lift. It's kind of an awkward thing. I mean, we're not exactly buddies or what have you, but I do think it's good, it's important, us getting to spend a little time one on one."

"Yeah, it's pretty sweet."

He went on. "Like it or not, we are, in our way, a family now, the four of us, and I'd hate more than anything for my presence to threaten you, or in any way—"

"You don't threaten me, Barry," I told him. "I just don't like you all that much."

He went quiet and gave a big sigh. "Wonderful. That's a terrific attitude you've got there, Ed."

Barry sank slowly back in his seat. I put the radio back up loud and went fast through the dark.

At the foot of a low grade, we came upon a restaurant that was a log cabin with some neon in the windows. Barry had kept up a pouting silence for about the last forty minutes, which got to me nearly as bad as his nasal, superior voice.

"Hey, back there," I said, with determined cheer. "I'm making a coffee stop. Feel like a bite?"

"Fine," Barry mumbled.

I pulled in. Marie and I set off across the parking lot. The night air was thick with the smell of the grease locker by the kitchen door. Barry took his time limping after us. Marie and I found three seats at the bar. The restaurant was a jolly place, with lots of crap hanging from the knotty pine paneling: iron farm tools, framed newspaper pages of football victories, license plates, and several stamped tin reissues of vintage advertisements with grinning, red-lipped black people on them. Wherever memorabilia wasn't, the locals had stapled up dollar bills scrawled over with marker scribblings. Before I could stop her, Marie reached out and tore one off the square support pillar beside her stool. The cocktail waitress saw her do it. She was a high-waisted girl with a scooped collar showing a big freckled cleavage. I took the dollar from Marie and held it out to the girl. "Open your mouth, and she'll take your fillings," I said. "Please don't call the cops."

The girl laughed. She cupped a hand to her face. "Keep it," she said. I thought I might get a line going with her, but she glided off with her tray, and Barry Kramer hobbled in. He didn't look at me but sat down beside Marie. He ordered a grilled cheese, onion rings, and a red wine, which came in a little bottle with a screw top. He started eating the pretzels in a dish on the bar while he waited for his food to come.

In the meantime, the bar was filling up with people getting unwound in a hurry. Some bank-teller-looking women in rayon suits were pouring tequila into themselves and sucking limes. In one corner, a kid in yellow sunglasses had set up a DJ rig, which was playing some bass music, and a buddy of the DJ's slid out onto the dance floor, each part of his body doing its own jittery urban dance. After a while, the bank tellers teased one another off their stools and went to try to have some fun with the dancing boy, but he cruised past them like they were traffic pylons, gone in his moves.

Down the bar, a small man in a pink golf shirt was having a beer and watching the television bolted over the back bar. He couldn't have been much past twenty-one. He looked extremely pissed and Greek, with a long nose and a half an inch of forehead between his brow and widow's peak. After a while, a big rangy girl came in and sat beside him. He didn't look at her, though everybody else did. About six two, she was a bleached giraffe in tight jeans and more makeup than a girl her age needed to wear. She put her elbow on the bar, propped her cheek on her fist, and blew an angry wad of air at the little man. The kid sucked his beer and pretended not to notice her.

"I was waiting for you at the house," she said.

"Yeah, I'm not at the house," he said, his eyes stuck on the TV.

"No shit," said the girl. She picked up a cocktail straw and used it to root around under her nails.

Our food came. I chopped up Marie's cheeseburger into little pieces. She would pick up each chunk of burger and lick it before she put it in her mouth. I'd never seen anybody eat like that before. For her dessert, I got her a piece of pie, which she pried two cherries out of and turned over to me. I ate it in three bites. It was late already, and we still had two more hours of dull, straight road between here and home.

But Barry took forever with his grilled cheese. He'd slowly drag it through a pool of mustard on his plate, take a bite, and

chew it for about ten minutes before swallowing. He eaves-
dropped on a joke a housepainter three stools down was telling
and laughed loud at the punch line. He watched the bartender
do a trick where he laid an empty bottle on the edge of the
counter and smacked the neck with the flat of his hand so the
bottle tomahawked in a high arc and landed in a trash can in
the corner. Barry and everybody clapped, except the young couple down the bar. The man's dinner had showed up. When the
woman tried to take a bite of his sandwich, he shoved the plate
at her.

"Knock yourself out," he said.

"What's your goddamn deal tonight, Lewis?"

"Nothin'. Just thought it might be fun to eat a meal one time
without your fuckin' hands in my food, but hey."

The waitress went by, and the boy called out to her. "Hey,
Jenny. Your tits look happy tonight."

"Yeah, well they're crying on the inside," she told him over
her shoulder.

The tall girl glanced at the waitress and then back at the boy.
"Let's go over to Cherokee," she said. "Don and Lisa are playing
cards."

"Enjoy yourself," he said, "and tell that asshole he owes me a
compressor hose." He slapped a bill on the bar and walked out
with his beer. The girl rolled her eyes like she didn't care, but
before the door had settled in the jamb, she got up and went after him.

They were out there in the parking lot when we made our
way back to my car. Things had escalated some by then. She had
the guy backed up against a blue GMC pickup, her finger in his
face, hair flying. I hoisted Marie and walked fast to the car, and
the couple went on with their loud words.

I strapped Marie in. Then I put the seat forward for Barry,

but he stood with his back turned, his eyes on the unhappy pair.

"You coming, Barry?"

He didn't move. The show was getting good. Barry watched the kid try to sidestep his big girlfriend and get in his truck, but she kept yelling and staying in his way. He shoved her chest and put her on her ass.

"Jesus Christ," Barry said. "We've got to do something here."

"What we need to do is get out of here and let these young people do their thing in private."

He screwed up his face at me. "You know, Ed, I feel sorry for you. I really do."

The woman didn't stay down long. A second later, she was up, whipping yards of white arm at the little man. He reached up and slapped her. The sound came to us with a tidy crack, like a baseball striking a mitt.

"My God," Barry said.

He spurred himself toward the kids on his crutch. I got in the car and cranked it, thinking to put him off his mission, but he kept on.

When Barry was about in spitting range of the couple, he came to a stop, blue light from a flood lamp spraying down around him in a bright cone. At the sight of him, they stopped going at each other. Barry started to speak in a tranquil Mendocino cadence, and for a time, at least, his California magic took effect. The kids shrank into themselves, suffering Barry's lecture like a couple of ninth graders caught sweating together under the bleachers. That meekness lasted about ninety seconds, and then the boy barked at Barry and feinted with his fist. The kid didn't reach his Adam's apple, but Barry scuttled back on his crutch, hiding behind his spread fingers, afraid for his face.

Yet he didn't back off. The boy wanded his beer bottle, and

Barry held his palms up, playing out some movie in his head where he was the beloved man of peace. In one way, I really did want to see that young Hilfiger golf hick take Barry's crutch from him and spindle him on it like a ballerina in a music box. But then, if Barry caught a beating, I knew it would make for a long resentment campaign from Jane, who'd surely hold me responsible.

I lifted Marie out of the shotgun seat and dropped her in back. Then I drove fast across the parking lot and rolled the window down and called Barry's name. The boy addressed me, bobbing on the balls of his feet in a near levitation of adrenaline.

"You got a problem, faggot?"

I smiled at him. "Not at all, shithead," I said. "Just need to grab my pal, and then you can get right back to beating on your girlfriend here."

The boy flung his bottle and it went to pieces on my door. Marie shrieked. A red fog pulsed in my vision, and I was out of the car, going for him. Barry put himself in my path, saying, "No, Ed, Christ, come on," and I stepped past him. The little Greek was grinning in a fraud of bravery, hoping, I suppose, that his put-on murder face would scare me into forgetting the four inches and sixty pounds he was giving up. The anger yawned big and hungry in my chest, and I knew not to let it go too far, just hit him on the nose once or twice. Maybe take his belt off of him and stripe him a little bit. I squared up and raised my hands, and then I was in a dream. It was of a dinner party at Jane's parents' house in Memphis. A storm was howling outside and lightning crackled in the windows. I was talking with Jane's father. "Better knaves than fools, Edward," he was droning. "Better knaves than fools."

I woke up on my back with a pain in my jaw. The little fellow was under me, wrapped around me in a complex whole-body grasp, some wrestling-team science I couldn't get loose from. His legs hooked both my knees. He had one arm on my throat, and he was using his spare fist to club at my temple. Above the blows and the breaths, and the little pivot noises of our striving in the dirt, was the nasal Klaxon of Barry's voice, bawling for help, when all he'd have needed to do to put an end to this was ram that crutch nub between the boy's straight white teeth and lean on it.

The young shit had me in a helpless way. I couldn't move or draw a breath. My eyes ran with frustration and pain. I was thinking there wasn't much to do but lie there and get knocked out, when, lo, I looked down and noticed the boy's face in a handy spot, right alongside my ribs. I raised my elbow and brought it down. He cussed weakly. I went again, and that second blow threw his master switch. He let out a sigh, and his grip around my throat relaxed. On the third stroke, something gave, and I felt it in my elbow, a queasy collapse, like a raw chicken bone yielding to the shears. The girl was yelling, kicking at me, and then someone pulled her back. By now, a small crowd of concerned citizens had spilled out of the restaurant. I rolled off the kid, and I didn't hear him even sigh.

I spat something hot and thick that didn't clear my chin. I tried to stand, but the man I'd seen behind the bar came and put a hand on me. "You stay put," he said. In his hand was a junior-size aluminum bat. I sat in the dirt near my bumper. Barry wasn't in the crowd and neither was Marie. The tall girl went to her friend, moaning over him, cradling his head. It was hard to look at, how his cheek sagged away from his eye.

The wheedling of my car door buzzer stopped, and I supposed some Samaritan had pocketed my keys. I tried to see who it was, but the bartender touched his boot to my leg. "How about you don't move until the cops get here?"

"He swung first," I said.

"And you went last. Bunch of times, it looks like. You stay there."

That was fine with me. I didn't really feel like going anywhere. I lay back, trying to breathe slow, my windpipe feeling like someone had crammed it full of embers. I closed my eyes. I could feel the strangers around me, and the blood howled in my ears. I needed to get my story together, needed to think what might be done with Barry and Marie if the police decided to hold me overnight, but all that seemed far away.

What came into my head right then was the memory of those nights when Jane would have her dreams. Sometimes the dream would infect me, too. I'd wake up screaming along with her, almost seeing that man with us in the room, knowing just a thin second stood between a hammer or a hatchet and the back of my head. She'd get up, cut the lights on, check the closets, under the bed, and I'd get up and do it with her, and not because she asked me to. When we finally got back under the covers, we'd stay up a long while in the dark, half sleeping, hearts going, conscious of all the places in our house where we hadn't thought to look.

LEOPARD

Good morning.

You have not slept well. Don't open your eyes. Stick out your tongue. Search for the little sore on your upper lip. Pray that it healed in the night.

No luck. Still there, rough to your tongue, and though it's very small, not even the diameter of a pencil eraser, it feels much larger. Your mother says it's a harmless fungal infection, and she pities you less for it than she should.

It tastes better than it looks. A tiny hamburger is what the fungus resembles, cracked and brown and perfectly centered in the little fluted area between your septum and upper lip. Yesterday, in the cafeteria, Josh Mohorn pointed out the similarity before a table of your friends. A painful thing, considering how much you would like to be Josh Mohorn.

He turned to you and said, "Hey, Yancy, do me a favor?"

"What's up," you said, excited by the rare pleasure of Josh's attention.

"Could you take that seat down there?" he said, gesturing at the far end of the table. "I can't eat my lunch with your fucking burger in my face." Even you had to admire the succinct poetry of the line, which launched an instant craze of everyone jeering and calling you "Burger King," or "Patty," or "All Beef," the name that stuck for the rest of the day and that will surely greet you this morning at school. You are eleven years old, the age when our essences begin revealing themselves, irremediably, to us and to the world. Just as Mohorn is irremediably a soccer ace and a clothes ace, with feathered hair and white buck shoes, you are irremediably a fungus man.

Don't go to school today. Play sick.

Your mother comes in to wake you. Around the house, she wears paint-spattered jeans, and old T-shirts through whose slack sleeves you often catch sight of her underarm hair. But this morning she is dressed for work in a blue sateen blouse and tight white slacks, clothes that speak of a secret life. "I don't feel good," you tell your mother.

"Where? In your stomach?"

"Yeah," you say.

"Oh, God," she says. "I hope it's not that thing that's been going around."

"I don't know what it is," you say, panting shallowly. "It just really hurts."

She puts her hand on your forehead and holds it there. Her palm is dry and cool. You have always admired her hands—long, thin fingers and clean, ridged nails that never need polish. On her right index finger knuckle is a perfect red dot, like a stamp of quality from the manufacturer. She slips her fingers down to your chest. Your skin is slick with sweat. You slept in your school clothes, jeans and a windbreaker, as you always do, amid the rustling mess of books and magazines piled in drifts on your bed. You will be twelve next year, but you usually still enjoy the solid, imperturbable sleep of a small child. You could get eight hours of good rest in a crate.

Your mother's fingers graze your sternum, and this makes you uncomfortable. A spray of large and painful pimples has recently sprouted there. They throb with humiliated awareness when your mother touches them. This area of your body is a source of worry, in part because, years ago, a babysitter told you that in their teenage years all boys develop a soft spot in their chests, like a baby's fontanel, and that you could kill somebody by punching him in that place. The babysitter was quite a liar, you realize now, even worse than you. He told you that in Florida there lived a race of murderous clowns who carried kitchen knives and who would come after you if you committed a sin. He also said that doctors performed abortions by delivering the baby and then putting it in a bucket and letting it cry to death. Still, you are not sure whether the babysitter was lying about the soft spot. The idea of it intrigues you. You writhe away from your mother's hand.

"What, you want to stay home?"

Swallow again. Close your eyes. "I don't know. I guess."

"Okay."

She kisses you and stands, ducking her head so as not to bash it on the top bunk, which is stacked with old blankets and boxes of your mother's stuff. She is right to be careful. Not long ago, you hit your head on it so forcefully that a hard white light went on behind your eyes. In your fury, you attacked the bed with your survival knife, inflicting minor, unsatisfying wounds. The little chips and gouges in the frame are a dispiriting reminder of the pointless assault.

On the shelf behind your head sits the tape deck your father bought you for your tenth birthday. You have stacks of cassettes full of your favorite songs, recorded off the radio, so all of them start a few seconds in, but you don't mind. You'd like to listen to your tapes, but you can hear your stepfather moving around in the kitchen. He is raising a din of clanking pots and clumsy feet, so loud you figure he must be doing it on purpose. You don't touch the tape deck because you don't want him to know you're awake.

He and your mother live on twenty acres in thick woods. Your stepfather fancies himself a kind of socialist frontiersman, and he doesn't have a normal job. He is too busy tending the three large gardens on the property, and splitting logs for the wood-burning furnace he persuaded your mother to buy. He values hard work above everything, and every time you turn around, your stepfather is there, putting a broom in your hand, or giving you a load of wet laundry to hang up, or telling you to fetch firewood, or scrub a sink, or dig a hole. "I have a job for you" is your stepfather's catchphrase, and you sometimes imitate it to make your mother laugh.

You rub your thumb along the soft white flesh of your forearm, which is still discolored from a job you had to do last summer. Your stepfather made you clear about an acre of honeysuckle, scrub, and vine where he wanted to put a shed. Halfway into the job, when he and your mother were away, you doused the jungle in paint stripper and set it on fire. You were careful to keep the hose handy, and the blaze didn't get out of control. You knocked out three days of work in one hour of fire. But the smoke covered you, and two days later you had poison ivy in a monstrous way. Blisters popped out on your hands, neck, and eyelids. Then they broke and crusted over into a multitude of little brown jewels. The doctor said it could have killed you if you had breathed the smoke. When you heard that, you were sorry you hadn't taken a lungful or two: not enough to do you in, but you liked the idea of having to spend some time in an oxygen tent because of a job your stepfather had put you to.

If you say no to your stepfather when he asks you to drop everything to do some chore, this is known as "lip." "I'm sick of your lip," he says, or "I've had it with your fucking lip." He is a thin, delicate man with wire-frame glasses, but neither his slightness nor his way of talking like a corny Hollywood thug makes you any less afraid of him. He has slapped you a few times. Not long ago, your father stopped by to pick you up and your stepfather argued with him. He pushed your father down, and then he picked up a stone the size of a football and made like he was going to throw it at your father's head. But he just tossed it away and laughed. For many years to come, whenever you think of your father, the image of him cowering on the lawn, his hands clutching his skull in forlorn defense against the crushing stone, will be part of the picture. You are counting the days until you turn sixteen, which you've arbitrarily chosen as the age at which you'll be able to take your stepfather in a fight.

At 12:30, you hear the front door creak and slap, and then the hornetish whine of your stepfather's leaf grinder starting up. Again, he is making mulch, a substance he seems to prize over food or money. Now it is safe to get out of bed. You go into the kitchen and pour yourself a large bowl of cornflakes. Take it into your mother and stepdad's bedroom, which contains the only television in the house. You are delighted to find *I Dream of Jeannie* on one of the U channels. Jeannie is miffed because, as an engagement present, Major Nelson's friends have crammed the house with the artwork of a terrible genius, sculptures that gurgle with digestion sounds. Barbara Eden's belly excites you enormously. You grope into your underwear. Almost immediately, you hear the leaf grinder power down. You turn off the TV, run into the kitchen, and arrange yourself at the table. Your stepfather comes in, trailing a rich vegetable aroma. Bits of leaf and bark cling to his glistening arms and chest. "Feeling better?" he asks.

"Not really," you say.

He claps a rough hand to your forehead. His hand smells deliciously of gasoline. "You don't feel hot to me."

"It's my stomach that hurts."

"You puke?"

"No," you admit.

"You must be feeling better or you wouldn't be having that milk. If you're ready for milk, you must be getting better."

You don't see what milk has to do with anything, but you don't want to argue with him.

"I've got a headache," you say. "I thought I should eat something is all."

He sneers suspiciously and snorts through his nose. As a young liar, you can generally get pretty far on the assumption that adults have more important things to worry about than catching out a kid for every little fraud he tries to pull. But your stepfather seems to have plenty of time to study and doubt everything that comes out of your mouth. He will spend days gathering evidence to prove that those are your teeth marks on a pen you said you hadn't chewed. Your hatred of your stepfather is all-consuming and unceasing, but this is only because your world is still small, and your stepfather assumes an outsize significance in the story of your life. That your stepfather seems to dislike you with an energy and relentlessness to match your own seems proof that your mother is married to a petty and dangerous child.

"You should get some fresh air," your stepfather says. "How about you go get the mail?"

This is not fair. The driveway is a half mile of rutted gravel that takes fifteen minutes to walk, and as far as your stepfather knows, you're sick.

"Why? Mom'll get it when she comes back for lunch."

"You go get it," your stepfather says. "The air'll be good for you."

"Actually, I'm still a little dizzy."

"I'll bet a hot fudge sundae you survive."

You set off across the lawn in bare feet. The earth under your toes is plush with mole tunnels. It is a hot autumn day. The clarity of the sky makes the trees look like television props with a blue screen behind them. You've already lost your summer calluses, and the driveway gravel is sharp, causing you to walk with a jouncing, high-elbowed gait like a bird trying to take flight. You blame your stepfather for the unpleasantness of the gravel, and every few feet you pick up a handful and fling it into the woods, hoping that those handfuls will cost a lot of money to replace.

You pass the woodpiles and the chicken house. Past the stretch of woods where you once built a handsome lean-to encircling the bottom of an oak tree. It was a pretty good one, made of windfall limbs peeled smooth with a draw knife and thatched with pine straw. One day, a boy from the new neighborhood on the far side of the woods showed up, and you had words. The next day you found the lean-to's ribs scattered across the clearing and your cache of untempting snacks—raw cashews, banana chips—emptied in the dirt. You mentioned the vandalism to your stepfather, and on a Sunday morning, when the boy and his family were at church, the two of you hiked through the woods and destroyed the expensive tree house on the boy's parents' property. Your stepfather tore off the roof tin and smashed the ladder with a crowbar. You broke the glass windows with stones, and you ached with the power of it—the two of you together in the same wild, righteous tribe.

You open the mailbox. It's crammed solid with magazines, bills, catalogs, and advertising circulars displaying red galleries of grocery-store beef, the sight of which makes the sore on your lip pulse. There must be fifteen pounds of mail, a sliding load that no sick person should have to carry. On the top of the heap, something catches your eye. It is a handmade flyer with a Xeroxed photo of what appears to be a leopard. "Lost Pet," reads the flyer, with a phone number below. A breeze starts down your neck. You turn and look into the woods, though you can see nothing. The leaves have not fallen yet, and you can't see twenty feet. You turn back to the flyer. The leopard looks scrawny and unfearsome, but your heart beats a little bit harder knowing that it might be out there, moving in the dull pine wastes near your home, its spotted paws treading silently over the tree roots, the pine needles, and the leaf-covered troves of ancient beer cans and patent medicine bottles, strewn there by careless people of the past. With the leopard out there, the woods seem famous now.

Far up the driveway, you can once again hear the whine of the leaf grinder starting up, a noise of startling crudeness and stupidity, an insult to the tickings and subtle movements of the living forest all around you. If this leopard is out here somewhere, it is surely offended by your stepfather's desecration of the silence. It would be no trouble for a leopard to sneak up behind him and carry him off, leaving no trace.

It is nearly one o'clock, the hour when your mother comes home for lunch. You do not want to be alone in the house with your stepfather. It still angers you that he has sent you down the driveway on your sick day, your special day of rest. You take a dozen steps, and then a plan suggests itself. Very carefully, you litter the mail in a haphazard fan on the driveway gravel so that it looks as though it were dumped there suddenly. You ease yourself down into a tire rut, splaying your arms and legs in the attitude of someone stricken by a fainting spell. When your mother's car swings into the drive, she will find you there. She may have to stand on the brakes to keep from running you over, but you are far enough up the driveway that you don't think she could hit you by mistake. She'll come to you crying and concerned. You'll let her coax it out of you, the story of how your stepfather made you get the mail.

Don't move. Don't mind the gravel digging into your cheek. Don't spoil the scene. She might not buy it anyway. Already, she halfway believes what your stepfather has been telling her about you: that you are a junior con man who can't open his mouth without a lie coming out.

An insect, probably a harmless black ant, troops up the back of your leg. Many minutes go by. As time passes, the giddy elation you felt at first at the brilliance of your stratagem begins eroding into shame. You decide you will wait until ten cars have rushed past on the blacktop road, and if your mother hasn't arrived by then, you will get up and walk back to the house.

It is the sixth car that you hear brake suddenly, reverse, and then roll into the drive. It is not your mother's car. It is a car with a large, smoothly whirring engine. Maybe it's UPS or someone turning around. Be still.

A door opens, and your tongue thickens hotly with alarm. You keep your eyes shut tight. Shoes with hard soles crunch toward you on the gravel. Someone leans over you.

"Whoa, buddy—hey, hey." It is a man's voice, high and nervous. A hand nudges your shoulder. "Come on, now, pal."

The man draws halting breaths. It startles you when warm

fingers find the side of your neck, searching for your pulse. Allow your eyes to open, taking care to flutter them as movie actors do when waking from a swoon. What first fills your vision is a shoe of gleaming black leather, possibly plastic, mounting to a gray trouser leg of synthetic fabric so clean and sharply creased it could have been cast in a mold. You glimpse the man's belt, where a large black pistol sits in a holster, and then up to the chrome badge on his clean gray shirt. He is young, his eyes bulging from a large, doughy face bracketed by blond sideburns that haven't filled in.

"Take it easy, now," he says. "Let's just take it easy."

If anyone needs to take it easy, it is not you but the policeman. His large head shifts in his collar, assessing the condition of your body with the edgy scrutiny of a rooster tracking a beetle. "You okay?" he asks again. "You in pain? You bleeding anywhere?"

"I—I don't think so."

"You live up there?"

"Yeah, yeah, I'm fine," you say. You sit up. The policeman puts his hand on your shoulder.

"Easy." He rubs his eye. "Jesus. You gave me a hell of a scare, buddy. I saw you and then that mail all scattered around. I thought, Oh, goddamn. I thought maybe I had a drive-by shooting on my hands, or at least a hit-and-run. Look at this," he says, presenting his hip to show that he's undone the holster snap that keeps his pistol in place. He seems too young and nervous to be trusted with a gun.

He asks how you're feeling and whether you've had fainting spells before.

"No, I'm fine," you tell him, getting up. "But thanks and everything." Begin gathering the mail. With any luck, he'll get

back in his idling cruiser and leave. Your mother will be return-
ing any minute. There isn't much time to jog up to the bend
in the driveway, out of sight of the road, and reassemble the
spectacle.

The policeman puts a thick hand on your arm. "Come on.
Come on in the car and get cool."

With the policeman's help, you gather up the envelopes and
catalogs. He ushers you into the passenger's side of the cruiser
and slants each of the dashboard vents so that they are all blowing at you. He races the engine. The breeze pouring from the
dash is sumptuously cold and laced with a faint hint of medicine
smell, like the waiting room of a dentist's office. Nothing your
mother owns smells bright and clean like this.

Jutting up from the dash is a shotgun in a metal brace. Scattered on the bench seat are other police tools—a big black flashlight, a notepad in a vaguely martial leather case. Somehow,
these things are more genuine and frightening than the shotgun, whose exact resemblance to what you've seen in movies
makes it seem unreal.

"You feeling okay?" he asks you. "Not dizzy or nothing?"

"No," you say. "I'm fine now. Totally."

"What's this thing here?" he asks, pointing at his lip to indi-
cate the hamburger.

"I had that before. It's just a fungus."

The policeman looks at you for a moment. His nostrils rise
in distaste. Then he unhitches his radio. "Two-oh-five, two-oh-
five," he says. "You can kill that call to Roger's Road. It's just a
kid who got a little dizzy and passed out. It's copasetic now," he
says, winking at you, though you are not sure why. It occurs to
you that you despise him a little for being so easily fooled.

The policeman goes on talking. "Tell you one thing," he continues. "I won't need my coffee break this afternoon. After seeing you lying there like that, I'll be keyed up all day. I mean, damn, I was sure we had another dead kid on our hands."

Your ears prick up at that word: "another." Last spring, Samantha Mealey, a nine-year-old girl from your elementary school, was found naked in a maple tree on the public golf course, a length of clothesline knotted around her neck. In fact, you'd met her at the bus stop just a few weeks before she died. She'd been a brassy, fearless little girl with a hoarse, appealing laugh. On that afternoon, much to the chagrin of her older brother, she'd been trying to pull some boys' pants down and cussing out loud for fun. She was an exciting girl.

You have not had your first kiss, but you are already worried about sex. Just two grades ahead of you, kids are having it already. When you learned that the man who killed Samantha Mealey had raped her before he tied the noose around her neck, what occurred to you was this: *At least she didn't die a virgin*—a thought you cannot share with even your wickedest friends.

You feel a manic impulse to start talking, to spare yourself from being alone with thoughts of Samantha Mealey's murder. You show the leopard flier to the policeman. "Have you heard about this?" you say. "There's a leopard running around out there."

He accepts the sheet and looks it over.

"Somebody had it for a pet," you say.

"See, I do not know who would have this thing at their residence, but I'll tell you one thing for sure: they're probably a dangerous element."

"Drug lords," you say.

"Could be. Bikers, maybe," the policeman says. "I swear, this whole area's changing. You just don't know anymore. Used to be this was a nice little town. Now it's turning into one of these places where anything can happen."

He passes the flyer back to you. You reach for the door. "So, thanks," you tell the policeman. "I should probably get going. My dad's probably wondering where I am." You pull the door handle. It's locked.

"Oh, you ain't walking anywhere, buddy," he tells you with a stern fondness that makes you uneasy. "I'll drive you. You keel over again, knock your head, I'm in real trouble."

He puts the cruiser into drive, and the car rolls forward. Untrimmed thorns and sapling limbs clutch at the car with intermittent shrieks that embarrass you.

"Thanks," you tell the policeman once the house pulls into view. "Thanks for the lift and everything."

He turns in the direction of the leaf grinder, where your stepfather stands with his back turned. "That your dad?" he asks. "Probably ought to talk to him," the policeman says. You don't want him to, but there is nothing you can do.

Together, you and the policeman walk across the lawn to your stepfather. The lawn is choked with a special weed that explodes seeds when you touch it. Little clouds detonate around the policeman's shiny shoes and land in his trouser cuffs. Your stepfather keeps feeding leaves into his grinder until the policeman is about three feet away. Then he turns. He narrows his eyes at the policeman, and then at you. The sweat is pouring off him, curling the hair on his bare chest into dozens of dark whorls. He turns the grinder off, looking hostile and put out.

"Who are you?" he asks.

"Officer Behrends, sir. I was driving past and I found your son lying in the driveway. He gave me a real scare."

"Hm." Your stepfather turns to you. The muscles around his eyes are tense. "What were you doing lying in the driveway?"

"I don't know," you say. "I just got dizzy and then I woke up. I guess I passed out."

"That mail was all scattered around and he was lying on his face," the policeman says. "I didn't know *what* had happened to him. He gave me a scare. I was thinking maybe he'd been shot."

"Maybe you sat down and then you fell asleep," your stepfather says after a moment. "That's probably what happened."

"I didn't sit down," you say. It is just like him to question your story, even with an officer of the law beside you, corroborating it. "I fell."

Your stepfather takes your chin in his thumb and forefinger and turns your face back and forth, as though it were a piece of merchandise he was thinking about buying.

"You must have fallen pretty easy," he says. "When you faint, you go down hard. You don't have any cuts."

"I don't know how I fell," you say. "I wasn't there watching."

"All right. Go inside, now," your stepfather says.

But you don't move. You don't want to. The sun slips behind a cloud. Something—you don't know what—is about to happen. You feel it, and you stand there, holding the mail, scraping the sharp edge of a magazine against your chin, out of which a single precious hair has lately dared to curl.

"Hell of a lucky thing that I saw him when I did," says the policeman. He seems to be angling for a handshake or words of gratitude from your stepfather, and you pity him for that. "Who knows? Somebody could have pulled in quick and run him over. It's a lucky thing."

"Yeah, pretty lucky," your stepfather says. Then he turns to you. "Go on inside. Wait for your mother."

But you stay where you are. Then, off in the trees behind the clothesline, you hear a branch snap, and the sound of something big tussling in the wooded shade. Your breathing goes quick and shallow. You close your eyes. Picture it, the leopard, its shoulders rising and falling as it lopes across the lawn.

"Hey," your stepfather says, lightly slapping your cheek. "What's the matter with you? Blacking out again?"

Don't answer. Listen. Be still.

DOOR
IN YOUR
EYE

My daughter, the very first night I was in her house, she wanted right off to put me in a state of fear. I was not even through with my soup when she came out, very excited, with a stack of photographs. She had them in a plastic Baggie so they'd be safe even in a flood. What was in those pictures she needed to be so careful about? Somebody lying dead in the street in front of Charlotte's apartment, shot in his chest, a black man about eighteen years old. "See, Dad? Right in here? See the blood dripping out of his mouth? That's how fresh he was when I found him."

"So what?" I told her. "It's a dead man. Do I know him? There's not enough terrible stuff around, I have to look at this?"

But my daughter was so excited about her photos, she made me go through every single one, all the way until we hit the pictures where the police and ambulance drivers arrived and spoiled her angle with their barricades. "After here it's no good," she said, pulling down her mouth. "You can't see anything. They blocked me out before I could actually see rigor mortis."

"You saw too much already, Charlotte," I said. "You never should have seen it, and then you turn around and show it to me. Some idea of how to make somebody feel welcome."

She knocked the stack of pictures hard against the tabletop to even them up. Then she slipped them back into the plastic bag. "I'm just saying it's not like Pottsville. You have to be careful here."

"I'm not afraid of this place," I said. "I've seen some things. I've been around the track a few times." If anything, I was afraid of my daughter, a grown woman who when she finds a dead man, the first thing she does is take a hundred photographs. I said nothing. Charlotte is a single girl, though she was married once. We threw her a big foolish wedding with tailcoats and a white limousine and a bagpiper walking around. Her marriage held on for ten months. Since then, Charlotte has gone to one school after another, hoarding up degrees, this latest one in public health. I didn't see her getting married again. She was forty-one. Her face was still a little bit pretty, but she'd turned into one of these girls who carries a big load under her belt.

"I hate to say it, Dad, but you're naive," she said. "Things happen all over this city, and you never know where. This is a risky place."

"So what? I just stay in the house all day, afraid for my life?"

"Of course not. There's plenty of good places for you to go. There's the Mintz Center on Nashville Street. They have games there, and cards, and I think they'll give you lunch and they don't charge."

"I'll go see about it," I said. "What kind of girls are there?"

"Old ones, I guess," she said.

"I don't mind," I said. "Maybe I can do some courting. Get myself a nice girlfriend."

"Oh, yeah? Been studying the pickup books? Getting your method down?"

"Hell, no," I said. "I don't have a method. My method is to be nice and congenial. Maybe you should try it."

My daughter turned away and went to picking at something on her big white arm. Charlotte didn't like to hear about me and girls. The whole reason she brought me down here was because of romance. I'd been mixing with a little Spanish girl in Pottsville. My daughter felt I was getting too romantic with her. So what? My wife was dead seven years, and there was no one else around.

I went back to my food, and this caused Charlotte to put her fingers in her ears and murmur to herself and look at her lap.

"What's your problem, sweetheart?"

"It's you and that soup. You tell everybody not to slurp, but I couldn't slurp as loud as you if I tried."

"Okay, fine," I said. "I'll take some dessert."

"There's some butter pecan," she said.

"Any Hershey's?"

"I think so."

"I'd like mine with some Hershey's, please."

She took my plate and walked into the kitchen, her heels clomping all the way. Everything sounded loud and strange in this apartment, because although Charlotte had been here two years, she did not have much furniture, and she hadn't put any carpets down.

Through the open window, I could hear more banging coming from across the street. A man was standing on an upstairs balcony, really giving it to the door. I undid the brake on my chair and turned it so I could have a better view. He pounded for a while, but no one answered. By the time Charlotte returned, the man was so frustrated that he was banging very hard on the tin downspout that ran along the edge of the house. This scared a row of little green birds from their perch on the power line. They swarmed around in the air, making hoarse calls. Apparently, the man had done this kind of knocking a few times before. The downspout was pretty beat up, bent and crimped like a stubbed cigarette.

Charlotte set the ice cream in front of me.

"Look at this joker," I said, pointing at the man with my spoon. "He's put himself in real trouble with his wife. She's got him out here knocking like an asshole, and she won't let him in."

Charlotte let out a little chuckle. "Ah. How apropos. That's no one's wife up there. That particular neighbor of ours," said my daughter in an important, sneering voice, "is a whore."

"Charlotte," I said, "what did this woman ever do to you that you have to be so ugly behind her back?"

"I'm not being ugly, I'm being honest," Charlotte said. "She goes to bed with men for a living. Just watch. She's got johns going in and out of there twenty-four hours a day."

As if to prove Charlotte's point for her, the door opened a crack right then. The man stopped his banging and slipped inside. The street went quiet and the green birds came back to the power line.

The next day, Charlotte went off to class, and I stayed in the house. I couldn't go to the Mintz Center. It would have been too much trouble for me. Even though Charlotte had said she was going to, she had not made the landlord come by and put a ramp on the steps. As a matter of fact, I don't really need the chair. I just like it for the purpose of saving energy, my energy. The way I look at it, if all I'm going to do is get up from where I'm sitting to walk to some other place just to sit down again, I might as well stay in the chair.

I keep a diary. I don't write anything in there except the weather, and I don't say a lot about that. "Warm, clear" is about the extent of what I put down. And with my little watercolor kit, I paint the sky. Not all the whole thing, only about as much as could go on a playing card. I used to put more words in the diary, but when I looked back on what I wrote, I noticed I'd become like a cheap newspaperman about my life, only telling unpleasant things—when I fought with my wife, or how much money I had given my daughter, or a time I was eating at a restaurant and a woman fell off her chair from a seizure. So I stopped writing words and decided to stick with just the paintings and the weather. It isn't much of a diary, but it's accurate, at least.

About noon, I went out on the porch with my kit. With the sun on my face, I ate the sandwich Charlotte had left for me, salami and mustard. Then I got to work. An unusual sky was happening that day. So much was going on up there, I had to make three paintings of it to get the whole idea across. Up above the power lines, it was pretty easy—just a simple blue. But down toward the Mississippi River there was a big green blackness with lightning going crazy in it, and this took some thought and care to paint correctly. Number three was the combination place of dark wisps where the storm clouds feathered into the blue.

I must have spent an hour making my three little watercolors, and in that time, three men visited the upstairs apartment of the lady across the street. One was a thin black man with a big beard and a Vietnamese peasant hat. Maybe the woman didn't like his looks, that hat or something else about him, because she made him whack the downspout for about ten minutes before she let him in. The second customer was a young white kid with baggy shorts and big pink calves. She didn't let him in at all. This signified to me that the woman was probably an interesting person. She wouldn't go with anyone. She had scruples of some kind. The third was a policeman in uniform, and he didn't have to wait but a minute. I got excited, thinking he was going to drag out the prostitute in handcuffs and I'd finally get a look at her. But no, fifteen minutes later the son of a bitch comes out by himself and drives off in his car. If I'd been a decent person, I would have taken down the license and called it in to the station. But for all I knew, the whole goddamned department was in on this kind of thing, and it would mean trouble if I called. Anyway, I stayed very curious about the woman. Each time she had a visitor, the door would open and the man would disappear inside with no sight of the lady. Not once did I even see her hand, and that was frustrating for me. It was like watching wind. You could only see her by what she moved.

After the policeman left, I waited for someone else to come along, but no one did, so I went inside and took a nap. Just as it was getting dark, Charlotte came home. We ordered in some Chinese for dinner, and then Charlotte said she was going to a dance lesson. To keep me occupied, she'd checked out some videos from the library, *The Thorn Birds*, which I'd already seen. Charlotte went to go dancing, and I didn't know what to do. I phoned up Sophia, the girl I knew in Pottsville, but there was nobody home.

At a quarter after nine, I got into bed. I fell asleep and what I dreamed was a true memory. I dreamed about Claudia Messner, a wild girl from my middle school. One time, she said she wanted me to kiss her in a cemetery, and I said okay. So we went into a cemetery. She picked out a nice big stone to sit on, and I kissed her on that. Her mouth had the flavor of a blackberry candy she was sucking on. After a little while, a young guy came by in a car. He said, Hey, you two can't do your kissing here.

What's it to you? I said, very tough.

Hell, I don't care, he said. But that's my uncle's stone and my aunt saw you two out here and it's making her nuts. She sent me to tell you to get off it.

So Claudia and me went to a little strip of forest right next to the highway and lay there in some vines until our lips were sore. It was a very nice memory for me. But I didn't get to dream the whole thing, because when my daughter came back from her dancing, she stuck her head in my door and said, "Hey, Dad, I'm home," as she used to do when she was a girl. It was dark in my room, and I still had Claudia in my head. I said, "Hello, Charlotte. I'd like you to meet Claudia, who's lying here in bed with me."

Charlotte didn't say anything. She just turned on the bright overhead light, looked at me blinking in my bed, and turned it off again.

My first week in Charlotte's house went pretty much like that first day. In the morning, my daughter would go off to school and leave me with a sandwich. I had no occupations. The watercolors and watching for the woman across the street—those were my occupations. The second fed the first. I wanted so much to see the woman that I stayed on the porch for many hours, doing my art. I painted not just my little samples of sky but everything I could see—the extra complex stuff they have on the power poles (you can't bury cable in this swampy town), the little houses, a giant pothole in the street, which people had tried to fill up with their garbage, including a broom sticking out of the hole to warn drivers. I painted a big dead rat in the drainage canal, bloated up so hard you could see its hide shining between its fur. Nearby, a crew of buzzards slunk around ignoring the carcass, as if to say, *We know we eat terrible things for a living, but there is a limit.*

I don't know how the woman stood all the work she was do-ing. Men to-ed and fro-ed along her steps all day and night, but in three days of watching, I still hadn't seen her. All I had to do was glance up at that door where a beige rag hung in the window, and my heartbeat would go a little quicker, and my temperature would heat up by a degree or two. What did she look like? Was she happy in there? Some men went in with packages. I won-dered if she got her groceries this way. Giving herself away for a chicken or a can of beans because she couldn't face her neighbors in the supermarket. Up and down the street, all day, I watched people coming and going from their houses. Only me and that woman I couldn't see were stuck at home. It was ridiculous, but I felt I had this connection with her because of that.

The fourth afternoon was a Saturday, and Charlotte said she wanted to make me a proper dinner of the last soft crabs of the season. She went off for groceries. I was on the porch when something happened that I could not believe. Somebody tried to burn the woman out. It wasn't a man I'd seen before. He had light skin, and a jacket with the Empire State Building in se-quins on the back. He did the ordinary thing of beating on the gutter, and when that didn't work, he took out a cigarette lighter and held the flame against the door. I should have yelled or called the police, but once again in life, I was a coward. You call the cops on somebody like that, and before long it's your house that's on fire. Panic, a sour tin flavor, came into my mouth. But I just sat there, watching him, doing nothing.

The man kept at it awhile, but he couldn't get the job done. He only put long smears of soot on the door. Finally, he quit try-ing, and he stormed up the street. I'd been an eyewitness to a felony crime, and I had an obligation. I rolled back into the house and I rifled around for something to write on. I found an envelope of Charlotte's from the gas company. On the back of it, I wrote, "Hello. My name is Albert Price. I am your new neighbor in 4903. I was a witness to someone trying to burn your door on Tuesday afternoon. I have his description." I put my daughter's number. Then I got out of my chair. I took up a cane, and I stepped out into the wind, which was blowing pretty strong. I crossed the street, no problem, but the steps to the woman's apartment were very challenging for me. When I reached the top, I'd run out of breath.

The idea was just to stick the envelope in the door and go away, but once I'd gotten up there, I had a hard time staying with the plan. I'd watched so many people try their luck on the door, it was as irresistible as a free roulette wheel. You had to give it a spin. I knocked. Nothing happened. I knocked again, a little harder. I was going to turn around when I heard footsteps inside. The door opened, just a crack. All I could see was an eye looking out of the crack, a large, nice hazel one. That eye had an interesting thing wrong with it. The pupil was enlarged and mis-shapen. It spread down into the hazel part like the hole for a skeleton key.

"All right," she said in a low voice. "What you want?"

I was caught off guard. I couldn't speak. I was still breathing pretty hard. "I live there," I said, gesturing down at my daughter's house. "Hell, I'm sorry. Here you go." I held the envelope out to her.

She looked at it without much interest. "You all right? You need a glass of water, or something?"

"To be honest, I could use one," I said. She opened the door. I glanced behind me at the street, but there was nobody to see me, just a dog sniffing at the storm drain. I stepped into her home and got a full look at her for the first time.

She wasn't the kind of hooker I was prepared for. She was an older person—younger than me, but she had plenty of years on her for that kind of trade. Her hair had gone silver, and it was knotted tightly at the back, proper as a Quaker woman. She had a smooth face and fine bones, and she wasn't wearing any garters or lace or bedroom stuff, just a clean white V-neck T-shirt and a blue jean skirt, showing off some very nice legs. I didn't know what to make of her.

There was a little hall, and then more steps. I took my time with them.

"You sure you're all right?" she said. "I hope you're not gonna keel over in here. This is a busy day for me."

"No, I won't. I could use that water, though."

She went into her kitchen and ran the tap. It was dim and cool as a basement in her place, which was just a room with a bed in the middle of it and a kitchenette to one side. On a table was an old sewing machine whose plastic had gone yellow. A quilt covered the bed, and it was cratered in the center where the woman had taken a nap, or maybe entertained somebody. A tomato plant stood by the window with one big red fruit on it.

She came back with the water, and I drank it in two slugs. "Need some more?" she asked.

"Yes, please," I said.

She filled up the cup and brought it back to me.

"Look, I just wanted to tell you, my name is Albert Price. I'm your neighbor. I live across the street."

"I know you do," she said. "You out there on that porch like you was afraid somebody's gonna steal it."

"Well, I'm sorry to disturb you, but there was a man out there just now. He had a cigarette lighter. He was trying to burn your door."

She made a clucking sound. "That's Lawrence," she said. "He thinks I owe him something, but I don't owe him anything."

"Maybe not, but he could have done you harm."

"I'd like to see him try," she said.

"*I* saw him try!" I told her. "He tried to burn down your house."

She closed her eyes halfway and shook her head. "Lawrence likes to make noise. He ain't really for real." She lit a cigarette, blew out a plume, and drew some of it in through her nose. "How old are you, Albert?"

"I'm eighty-three," I said.

Her brow went up and down.

"And you came all the way up here to tell me that?" She leaned against the wall and crossed her arms across her chest. "Just to tell me about Lawrence? Nothing else I can help you with?"

I needed to think. I'd never gone with a whore in my life, except one time, in Germany, a morale girl some buddies of mine snuck into the barracks. I don't think she was fifteen years old, and we all pitched in on taking her in terrible ways.

This was different, a grown woman. I thought about kissing her and my hands on her skin, and it came into my mind that maybe this would be the last woman I would ever get the chance to touch. What did it mean, I was wondering, to finish the count of women in your life?

My breathing was the loudest thing in the room. I didn't feel steady. "Could I sit down here?" I asked her. "Could I sit on your bed?"

"I don't mind."

"What's your name, miss?" I couldn't hear over my heart.

She stroked her throat with her fingers and took me in through half-closed eyes. "Carol," she finally said.

I reached out to put my water glass on the table. My hand was shaking so it made a loud noise when I set it down.

"That's a pretty name," I said, though I didn't particularly think it was.

"Thanks," she said. I could see that under her shirt, she wasn't wearing a brassiere.

"Okay, Carol. What if you were to just get down here next to me? I just want us just to lie here for a little while. What would be the price for that?"

A doubtful extra chin formed under her jaw. "What the fuck are you talking about, Albert?"

"I'm not up for much," I said. "I want us just to lie here. Now, I have twenty dollars in my pocket. I'll give it to you. Twenty dollars for just resting. To me, that seems like a pretty good deal."

Then Carol began to laugh a high, chiming laugh, a really pretty sound. I couldn't remember the last time I'd said something to make a person laugh this way. When she finally got control of herself, she said, "Hold up, Albert. You think I'm a *whore?*"

I said nothing, and she went into another laughing fit.

"Whore," she mumbled into her hand. "This will kill Glenda. This will break Glenda up."

"What?"

"*Pay me to lie down with you.*" She rubbed her palm against her eye. "You lucky I'm so easygoing, Albert. Most people, you come out your mouth with that, you'd be in some shit."

"If you don't want to, that's your business," I said, a little angry now. "Only please don't treat me like I'm stupid. I see the men coming in and out of here."

"Albert, you got it all fucked up," she said. "I don't sell this body."

"You don't?"

"Hell, no. I sell *drugs*."

"Oh, my God," I said.

"Shit, everybody on this street knows that. I sell to everybody. Even them people on the corner with the big house and that big iron fence."

I put a hand to my face. "Oh, Christ. I apologize."

"That's all right," she said. "You got confused."

"Oh, Jesus," I said.

"That's all right," she said. "You're up here, now, Albert. Now tell me, what kind of thing you need? I got sleeping pills, Vikes, Xanax, pills for your mood. They bring it up from Mexico. You spend more at the Walgreens."

"I don't need that stuff," I said. "I take a water pill. That's all."

"I got some gentle weed. Help you with your appetite. You better put on weight if you're trying to stay down here. It's not a town for skinny people. It's a town for the big set."

I thought it over. "You're talking about reefer?"

"Uh-huh."

"I'll tell you what, then. I'll buy a reefer from you."

"A joint?"

"Sure," I said. "A joint. What the hell."

"Come on, now, Albert. You can do a little better than a little old joint. I got some bills to pay."

"All I've got is this twenty. Does that buy a joint?"

I held up the bill.

"That'll work," she said, and took it. She reached under the bed and pulled out a plastic container that was full of bags of marijuana and pinched a little from one of the bags. Then she sat in a chair beside the bed. She had no rolling papers, so she emptied out a cigarette and began carefully tamping the stuff down the frail, empty paper.

"Can I ask you a question, Carol?" I asked.

"Depends on what it is," she said.

"What happened to your eye?"

"It don't work right. I can see light and dark and that's pretty much it."

"Sure, but what happened to it?"

She was quiet. "Impact," she said after a time. "Detached retina."

"Okay, so what detached it?"

She sighed. "Matter of fact, it was a bullet. From a .22 pistol. My husband shot me. That's what they say, anyway."

She held the joint out to me. It was a pretty crooked joint for twenty dollars. "You get it started, Carol."

She shrugged. "I'll take a little puff."

She put a match to the joint and drew in a deep lungful.

"So what do you mean, 'That's what they say'? You don't think he shot you?"

"To be honest, it's just as likely that I did it. I remember that gun in my hand at one point."

"I'd say you look pretty good for getting shot in your face."

"Well, I didn't look good when it happened. My eye swelled up like a basketball. And you know how they prop you up in a hospital bed? I was sitting like that, blood running down like this, and it ran across here and made a perfect cross. They brought all the nurses and orderlies in to see that cross, like it was a miracle. But I wasn't thinking about God in that hospital, and I don't think about him now."

She passed the cigarette to me. I took a pull on it. "What were you thinking about?" I asked her when I'd stopped coughing.

"I was just kind of tripping out on what getting shot is all about. How it's just you getting touched by a little thing, only it's touching you really fast. If it was going slow, you'd be fine as pie. The only thing matters is the speed."

It was quiet in the room, and then I said, "Funny you should have been shot."

She dipped her brow at me. "Yeah, it was funny as a mother-fucker."

"No, I mean, it's a funny connection for us, Carol. I've been shot, too."

"No shit?"

"No shit. In Germany. In the war. Here."

I pulled aside my collar so she could see my wound. It seemed to interest her. She leaned in and ran her fingers over the scar a couple of times, very tenderly. Then she pulled up my collar and smoothed it out with her hand.

"The Germans shot you?"

"Nope," I said. "It was my own sergeant. This was towards the end. We didn't have much of an outfit left, no artillery or heavy weapons, but for some reason, he wanted us to cross the Elbe River, where all the fighting was. I said we'd be an asshole to try to cross without laying down a barrage, and I wouldn't do it. Suddenly, behind me, a pistol goes off, and the guy shoots me. I said, 'God, am I here yet?' By the time I was healed up, Truman had dropped the bomb."

Carol smiled at me. Her teeth were very white and straight. "You a religious man, Albert?"

I tried to think this over, but I couldn't really focus my thoughts. I was pretty rearranged from the reefer. I shrugged my arms. The fabric of my shirt felt new against my skin, and I shrugged one more time for the feeling.

"Sure," I finally told the woman. "God's a wonderful person. I like him."

Carol laughed beautifully at this.

"You were right about this dope," I said after a while. "It does make you crave something to eat."

"You hungry?"

"Oh, yes," I said.

"Well, don't look at me," she said. "I can't be cooking now. This is one of my busy days."

"What about that?"

"What?"

"That tomato. We could eat that," I said. "It looks ripe."

"You want to eat my tomato?"

"Sure," I said.

She reached out and snapped the tomato off its vine and handed it to me.

"You don't want some?"

"Nah," she said. "Go to town."

I took a bite. It was delicious, full of the strong, green flavor of the vine. So much juice ran out that Carol stopped me and went to get a towel. The juice ran down my chin. I could feel my beard getting heavy with it, but I didn't care.

I was nearly finished when Carol motioned me over to the open window. Charlotte had gotten home. She was out on the porch next to my empty chair, holding the crabs in a white paper package, turning her head up and down the street.

"That your daughter?"

"That's her," I said.

Charlotte shouted out for me, a yell as loud as a bullhorn.

Carol seemed not to hear. She held up the little remnant of our cigarette. "You want any more of this?" she asked.

"No, thank you," I said.

She licked her fingers and pinched it out, and then she popped it in her mouth and swallowed it.

Down below, Charlotte yelled for me again. "You're not going to see about her?" Carol asked.

I put my hands on the windowsill and stuck my entire head out into the afternoon. The wind chilled the wetness on my lips and my chin. "Hey," I called out to my daughter. "Hey, Charlotte, look up here."

WILD
AMERICA

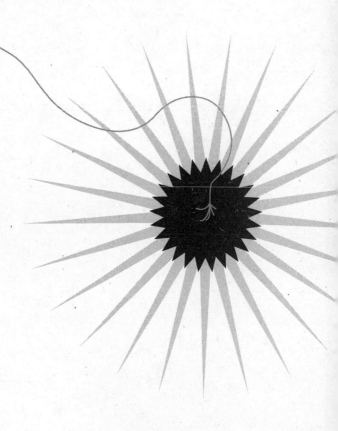

The bell on the cat's collar roused her. He'd brought her something: a baby pigeon stolen from its nest, mauled and draped on Jacey's pillowcase. The thing was pink, nearly translucent, with magenta cheeks and lavender ovals around the eyes. It looked like a half-cooked eraser with dreams of someday becoming a prostitute. Jacey screamed briefly, then got up and ran to the bathroom, shutting the door behind her to contain the cat in the room. Her hope was that the cat would eat the bird before she had to look at it again.

Eleven thirty. Her mother would be counting pills at the pharmacy until eight o'clock tonight. This left Jacey to spend the day with her cousin Maya, who was down here for the week. Four days ago, Maya had descended from the mountains to visit before going off to a free government school for the best young dancers in the state. In Jacey's opinion, Maya had already been here too long. As children, they'd spent nearly every summer together in joy. They'd suffered summer camp as a team, had stolen newts from mountain ponds and chocolate and lipstick from Charlotte drugstores and, in later days, some wine and painkillers from Maya's unhappy mother. They had tried out their first kisses on each other, just as practice, and one summer, when Jacey was ten, they'd eaten scabs from each other's knees to cement a pact to someday raise their families in the same duplex home on the Carolina coast.

But the bond of that scab lunch was no longer worth much when puberty hit and aimed the girls at different destinies. Three weeks shy of sixteen, Maya had evolved into a five-foot-ten-inch mantis of legendary poise and ballet repute, while Jacey still went around with a shiny chin and forehead and a figure like a pickle jar. Maya sighed a lot over Rudolf Nureyev and often said how hard it was to love a dead man. She worried about her art in language borrowed from New York critics—"It's so hard to find a balance between exactitude and passion"—talk as comprehensible to Jacey as whale song. She fretted over the precious cartilage in her knees and ankles, saying, "I'll never forgive myself if I have to fall back on modeling"—already, she'd appeared in local circulars for a chain of department stores.

It wasn't as if Jacey lacked gifts of her own. Her singing voice was a confident, husky alto that never strayed from key. At the junior follies, she performed the anthem "Strawberry Wine" with so much solitude and longing that the gym teacher, a white-haired gargoyle who'd never expressed a single sentiment besides "Muscles work by shortening," had had to dab away tears. So what? You didn't hear Jacey going on about how all of Manhattan or Nashville would be aching for her soon. No, she planned to plow on to a career in pharmacy or physical therapy, maybe sing a little around the house if she found a husband who could play a good guitar. Where Maya had been chosen to flit high above life's brambles, Jacey was not ashamed to be the honest little boulder, rolling bluntly through the thorns.

Though this would probably be the last summer interlude the cousins would share, Maya had shown insultingly little interest in spending time with Jacey. Here were things Maya had so far declined to do with her cousin: go ice skating at the mall, see a movie, attend a secret beer party two neighborhoods over, shop, and watch the volunteer fire department light a derelict house on fire and hose it out. Maya seemed to regard all the attractions of greater Charlotte as tiresome backwoods dullness — this from someone whose hometown consisted of railroad tracks, two dozen hicks and craftsfolk, and some dogs. What could you do with a person like that? You could not say another nice word to her until she left for dance school on Monday, which is what Jacey resolved to do as she made her way downstairs.

In the sun-warmed closeness of the room, Jacey sprawled across the daybed. The toasted, musty scent of the quilt was pleasant in her nose. Jacey decided she would be happy in this spot until her father arrived that evening and took her out to dinner. Every two weeks, he drove up to see her from where he lived with his wife in Southern Pines. Jacey was still recovering from the half decade of seething hostility she'd felt toward her father after her parents' divorce. During the worst of their difficulties, two years ago, Jacey had tried to stab her shy father with a nail file. This news had gotten out, and to this day Jacey's extended relatives viewed her as the family's embarrassing lunatic, bound for a life of poverty and disgrace, though Jacey was a responsible student and had made the A/B honor roll four semesters straight. There wouldn't be any more violence with her father. Hate is tiring when the fun wears out, and she lacked the energy for it now. Anyway, her father really hadn't done anything wrong except marry a tall, raucous woman whose stirrup pants matched her army-general bearing. Jacey looked forward to seeing her father tonight. She hoped to persuade him to take her to Crawdaddy's Restaurant, so she could have the Cajun Chicken Littles that she liked.

Jacey clicked the television on. It showed golf, golf, *Mama's Family*, and the program *Wild America*. The host Marty Stouffer was busy at his habit of laying bare hands on something horrid and fascinating from nature—today, a heap of freshly discarded velvet from an elk's horns. Veins were in the stuff. It looked like carpet from a murder site.

"Look at you, little cozy," Maya said when she entered the sunroom at a quarter of twelve. She was dressed in her latest style, a gauzy swoon of scarves and shawls in the mode of Stevie Nicks. In one hand she held a handkerchief, in the other a box of Vantages. Maya smoked openly. No one gave her trouble about it because in her profession a cigarette was seen as something like a vitamin. Maya yawned and began to twist her hair into a knot. It hung thick past her waist, and she complained about it often, usually declaring in the same breath how she planned to donate it to a company that made wigs for cancer patients. Really, it was a small miracle that Maya had not caught fire with all her gossamer swaddlings and surplus moral hair wafting near the embers of her cigarettes.

"There's a dead bird in my bed," Jacey said, not taking her eyes off the screen.

Maya looked quizzical. "What's that, code for something?"

"For a dead bird in my bed."

"Seriously? Right now?"

"Yep."

"What kind of bird?"

"Nasty," said Jacey. "An ugly wet little baby."

"Can I see it?"

"Nope," said Jacey.

"Why not?"

"Scopes is locked in there with it, is why. I'm not letting him out until he eats it."

"Aren't you clever," said Maya.

"Compared to what?" said Jacey.

Maya looked discomfited. She gave an awkward rear-throat chortle. Jacey thought with some glee that Maya was already feeling the sting of her indifference. As if seized by a sudden chill, Maya launched into a piping suite of sneezes. "Ex*cuse* me," she said. "Something around here is really giving me the snuffles."

Jacey flipped the channels through the whole loop and came back to Stouffer, still handling that awful velvet. "Hold your breath, I guess."

"Mm-*kay*," said Maya. "So you just left it there? The bird?"

"Yup."

"I'll throw it out for you, if you want. I don't mind dead stuff."

"Scopes is on the case," Jacey said. In the face of Maya's sudden gentleness, now Jacey felt small and childish. "Hey, you hungry?"

Maya said she'd love a bite of something, and Jacey went into the kitchen to whip up a large gourmet brunch for two. She forked cheddar cheese into some eggs, and with a butter knife, she pried a gray cube steak from the rink of ice tray sloshings at the bottom of the freezer. She threw that in the pan with a clang and goosed the flame until the meat bent and smoked. Then she doused it with a pour of red wine from an open jug.

"Oh, my God," Maya groaned over her plate, though the piece of beef she had accepted was no larger than a domino. "Jace, this is literally the best thing I've ever put in my mouth."

"Plenty left," Jacey said around a juicy mouthful.

"Ooh, better not," said Maya, which Jacey would have taken as an insult had Maya not winningly disclosed that as much as she loved red meat, it tended to strand her on the commode. Jacey finished the steak in good cheer while Maya rounded out her brunch with cashew butter spread thin across an oaten shingle, foods she'd packed down specially from the hills.

For three quarters of an hour the girls lay on the daybed in companionable style, talking of the habits of their mothers, both single ladies, and of the failings of their fathers and their fathers' wives. They talked of rock and roll, shampoo, and of a terrific new brand of wine cooler for sale at your better stores. Then Maya glanced at the brass pocket watch she was affecting these days. She said, "Ah, suck. Jace, do you think Aunt June would care if I called Charleston? I need to. I can leave her some bucks."

"Who's in Charleston?"

"Oh, this guy Doug"—a fellow model, Maya explained, with whom she'd been photographed last spring in a seaside embrace, an advertisement for the Big Stick Surf Shop in Myrtle Beach. Maya reached into the Guatemalan bag that was always close at hand, and produced a photograph of a tanned young man with a cowrie shell necklace standing on a beach. Teeth so white and even they looked false, eyes large and liquid as a mule's beneath dark and tousled salt-stiff hair. He was a person of such beauty that Jacey had to check the back of the photo to be sure it wasn't a clipping from a magazine.

"This is your boyfriend?" Jacey said.

"In his opinion," Maya said. "He's been up to see me a few times. He wants to take me to Burning Man in August. He's always talking about how you can get married in Nevada when you're sixteen. I can't say how many times I've told him no, but he keeps not getting the message on purpose. He's really kind of a pest."

Jacey was still gripping the photo. "Shit, Maya. There's people out there who'd cut off their foot to get with somebody that looks like this."

"Fine but poor, dumb Doug," Maya said with a sigh. "The other day, I was telling him about how I want to do the Peace Corps in Suriname, and he asked if there were any tigers left in Africa."

In Jacey's opinion, Maya herself was guilty of some idiocy here. You did not low-rate a racing stallion because its command of French was poor. But Jacey kept her mouth shut because she didn't know where Suriname was, either. If she had to guess, she'd have said it had something to do with the Vietnam War.

Maya cut her eyes at Jacey. "But actually, that's not why I need to ditch him. There's something else."

"What?"

"It's a secret. You gotta swear you won't tell."

"Sure," said Jacey.

"Not anyone. Not even what's-her-name, Dana."

"We're not friends anymore."

"Don't even put it in your diary. If Aunt June finds out, I am so seriously fucked."

"Shit, I *won't* already. Would you just tell me?"

The secret was this: Maya had been intriguing with Robert Pettigrew, an assistant director at the Governor's School of the Performing Arts, where Maya was heading next week. She'd met Pettigrew at a statewide competition in Lenoir the previous spring. They had been corresponding, and his letters had confirmed that he was a sincere and caring person who, despite their age difference, was, Maya said, "totally in touch with my world."

"How old?"

"He just turned thirty-five," said Maya.

"Jesus Christ! Did you say *thirty-five?*" yelled Jacey.

Maya's face grew cold and dark. She went for her cigarettes. "Forget it. Stupid to tell you."

"Look, Maya, I'm not gonna nark you out, but it's just, I mean, thirty-*five*."

"Judge me, I don't give two shits," Maya said curtly. "It's between me and Robert, and as far as I'm concerned, everyone else can cram it. Age is just a label. Our thing is, we're both old souls."

"Guess not."

Maya sighed. "I love him, Jacey."

There was no responding to this remark. Jacey's own father was merely thirty-seven.

"He just unlocks these *rooms* inside me," Maya was saying. "It's like he knows things about me that I don't even know myself."

In private revulsion, Jacey clenched her teeth so that an upper canine screeched against a lower. "God, well have you, I mean did you-all . . ." Jacey could not find a term appropriate for when a young girl is groaned on by a thirty-five-year-old lieutenant of the arts.

"Have we been lovers?"

Been lovers—the eyeteeth screeched again. Who said that? It called up an image of those two at it beneath a flowering arbor while swans watched. "Did you?" Jacey said.

"Robert wants to wait until Thanksgiving, until I turn sixteen."

"Wait for good, is my advice. I think you're insane to give up on Doug." Jacey was gazing at the photo, smoothing the hair with her finger. "*Suriname*. I'd take him if he couldn't find the earth on a globe."

Maya giggled into her teacup with a bubbling grotto sound. "Well, you're welcome to him, Jace. I can hardly stand to talk to him on the phone. After with Robert? Seeing how it can be? Even talking to Doug makes me feel so incredibly alone. When he talks, it's just sound. It's like the noise in a seashell."

"See, I love that sound! It's relaxing!"

"Then you guys would make a nice pair."

"Yeah, except he'd never like me," Jacey said.

"Trust me, Jacey, he'd be lucky to get you."

"Sure he would."

"Why not? You're beautiful. You're hot. I'd pay a million dollars to have your eyes and your sweet freckles. Believe me, you'd be selling yourself short. He wouldn't even get your jokes. You'd be instantly bored."

"That would not happen," said Jacey.

"You do the road trip with him, then. Four days with Doug will send me off the deep end. It really will."

"I'd go in one second."

Maya laughed her trilling laugh. "Fantastic. You'd be bailing me out in a major way."

"No, I'm serious!" said Jacey, now sitting cross-legged and straight-backed on the sofa bed, nearly quaking with interest. "I'm there."

"Okay, okay. Don't swallow your tongue. Anyway, I really do need to call him. You don't think Aunt June would mind?"

Jacey felt a little dizzy. "Hell, no!" she said, and ran off to fetch the cordless phone.

Maya looked a little put out that Jacey hovered so near while she dialed up Charleston. But Jacey, who was temporarily insane with fantasies of coasting through Nevada buttes in the car of Doug, the mule-eyed cowrie man, was not about to leave. She wanted to see what wiles and arts Maya would use to bring this thing about. Let him down easy, and then slip him Jacey as a substitute when the moment was perfect, that was the trick—like the moment in *Indiana Jones* when Jones swipes the golden idol off the weight-sensitive dais and swaps it so deftly for the bag of sand. A delicate maneuver, one that only someone like Maya with her grown-up, alien grace had the gifts for pulling off.

To her disappointment, Jacey could just barely make out the sandy rasping of Doug's voice in the receiver. She wished she'd thought to listen in from the extension in her room. Wisely, Maya did not launch straight into talk of Jacey but first lulled him with some chitchat. She talked about a chigger bite on her knee. Then she had some words to say about someone unknown to Jacey named DJ Now-and-Later. Then Maya started discussing the photo shoot for a Belk Leggett holiday mailer. By now Jacey was thinking it was probably time to get down to brass tacks on the issue of her trip to Burning Man. But the chatter wound on through another seven (probably expensive) minutes of friendly nonsense before Maya finally said, "I told you, Forgetful Jones, I'm not *at* home. I'm down near Charlotte, staying with Aunt June and my cousin Jacey."

Hearing her name, Jacey felt an exhilarating terror that Maya was going to put the phone into her hand. What could she say to such a man? Wild-eyed, she shook her head at Maya, who returned a bothered look and went on talking. Though Maya was more the expert in these matters, Jacey felt she could use some coaching at this point. She tapped Maya's knee. "What *is* it?" Maya whispered.

"Look, just say I'm funny," Jacey said.

"What?"

Jacey swallowed.

"Just tell him I'm funny and hot."

Maya nodded. "Yeah, Doug? Hey, I've got a message from my cousin. Yeah. She wants me to tell you she's funny and hot." Jacey felt an urge to barf.

"Of *course* she does, dummy." Maya cupped her palm over the receiver. "He says to tell you '*preesh*.'"

Jacey gaped at her cousin for a moment. Quitting the sunroom, she had to try hard not to break into a run.

Up in Jacey's bedroom, Scopes the cat had done nothing with the bird. He was hunched beside it on the pillow, settling in for an all-day gloat. Jacey scowled out her window. Her pulse drummed in her cheeks. She wished she had something valuable to smash. She heard Maya hang up on Charleston, and her breathing slowed a little. Then Jacey picked up the phone and called Leander Buttons at his parents' home.

Jacey had necked with Buttons ten days earlier. It had sort of been an accident, and Jacey's plan was not to talk to him until school started in the fall, if then. Leander wasn't much more than five feet tall. He was known behind his back as "Little Buttons," and sometimes to his face. He'd been homeschooled until eighth grade. A boy of mixed interests, he was good on the trombone and was also aspiring to be a burnout. His crowds included both the doofs of the marching band and those lesser hippies who kicked the Hacky Sack on the farthest circle of the school's doper scene. Little Buttons's hygiene was poor. His eyes watered, and he so often had a piece of food in the corner of his mouth that you wondered if he kept it in a bedside saucer overnight and donned it in the morning. One time at lunch, his friends took a set of clippers to his head, and the resulting ball of hair was a marvel of filth, full of so much natural grease that it held its form when kicked about the Hacky ring.

But there had been mitigating circumstances for Jacey to get close to him the other night uptown. That evening, Jacey had climbed high into the magnolia tree overreaching the New Life Church with her best friend, Eileen Gutch. They'd drunk three bottles apiece of Little Kings Cream Ale before a rough, hot rain began to fall. The weather sent Gutch running home. With two hours until her mother picked her up, Jacey was alone, woozy and heart-swollen in the downtown, wandering wet streets that gleamed as you would have them gleam in the sweet summer film of your life.

Down by the parking deck, she saw Little Buttons stagger from a shrub. They were not friends, but they had shared homeroom and English class two years in a row. His shirt was mulchy, and he had a red dome on his forehead. He explained he'd just now bashed it on something during a bout of "The Elevator," also known as "The Charlotte Classic," in which you hyperventilated and your friend rammed you on the sternum so that you fainted for a low-rent high. Leander's partner in the Classic had also vanished when the weather came. So in an act of beery tenderness and rainy-night desire, Jacey took Leander's hand in hers and led him to the planetarium. Not to the main theater, where you had to pay four dollars to watch the star machine throw the constellations—but to an old, free place, the Copernican Orrery on the forgotten second floor. Here, when you mashed a green lozenge on the wall, the lights dimmed, hidden gears in the ceiling thunked and squealed, and for five minutes the planets of the solar system, portrayed by foam balls spray-painted Day-Glo colors, lurched around a yellow party bulb that was the sun.

She and Buttons lay in there an hour and a half and mashed

the lozenge eighteen times. The necking got fairly grave, but nothing irreparable took place. At one point, Little Buttons quit his exertions to ask if Jacey was a virgin, a question she had no exact answer for. The story was this: Last summer, at a coeducational overnight camp in Tennessee, she wound up in a tent with a boy from New Jersey, also thirteen at the time. He went at her. His wooing was a literal impersonation of the ardent French skunk, Pepé Le Pew. Miraculously, this had resulted in both Jacey's first real kiss and her first mostly nude movements with a boy. For technical reasons, she had not wholly "given up the rock," as Eileen Gutch liked to describe the act. If she had to put a figure on it, Jacey supposed she'd given up the rock by about forty percent. So there in the orrery, she whispered "Not really" to Little Buttons, who was so stirred by this news that he began to breathe as though another Charlotte Classic was at hand.

Leander Buttons had telephoned three times the day after their solar system interlude and four times the day after that. Jacey had not called him back. Until this very morning, Jacey hadn't seen much value in being liked by a stray runt like Leander. But now with her intolerable cousin in the house, Jacey had the blues. She thought it might be good to have somebody, *anybody*, come by and like her for a while, no matter how much food he wore in the crook of his lips.

"Jacey?" came the high kazoo of Leander's voice over the phone.

"Yes, Leander."

"Wow. It's weird you're calling me," he honked. "I only left about fifty thousand messages."

"I'm sorry."

"You could've told me you made it home, at least. Somebody could have murdered you, for all I knew."

"Yeah, well, I did get murdered, but just a little. But listen, Leander, what are you doing today?"

"Not much. Practicing my trombone." He gave a little blurt as proof. "Then I told my sister I'd help her make a peanut butter log because she's bummed out and wants to cook. Then maybe duckpin bowling with Josh Gurskis and some dudes."

"I've got an idea. Don't do any of that stuff," Jacey said briskly. "Come over to my house. I want to have a movie day."

"At your house?" His tone was cautious. He seemed to smell a trap.

"Yes, Leander, at my house."

"With your parents?"

"No. No parents. My mom's away all day. She's at work."

"Um, well, what kind of movies are you talking about?"

"Let's see, there's at least *Jaws* and *Turner & Hooch* and I think *Excalibur* and one that I don't know what it is. The label's rubbed off."

"Well, what do you think that one is?"

Jacey sighed. "Shit, Leander, I don't know! But if it's been here this long, it's probably something good. Now, look, do you want to come over here or not?"

He said he'd be there in about one hour.

Little Buttons had to ride a Puch-brand moped eight miles to get to Jacey's house, which lay in a rear-county outbreak of brick ramblers on the verge of some state woods. Jacey ran downstairs when she heard the moped blat into the lane. By the time she was out the front door, Leander already had the kickstand down and was inspecting a ding in the Puch's blue flank.

"What's going on?" she asked.

"For one thing, I nearly got in a wreck coming over here. Somebody threw a Cheerwine can at me on Piney Mountain Drive."

"No way. Are you hurt?"

"Nah, it was just an empty can, but still, I almost drove into a tree. That fucker. He's lucky I was trying to get here fast, or I'd have followed him home so I could cut his tires sometime."

Honestly, Jacey could see how somebody might want to throw a can at Little Buttons. He was dressed to invite one. His hair was not the usual nest. Rather, he had slicked it back with so much styling crud, it looked like a knob of fresh pavement. His shirt was a nightclub shirt of a shiny fabric, and he wore tight black jeans that tapered to a pair of feathered loafers like something stolen off an Alpine pimp. In one way, she was flattered that he had taken the time for all that primping, yet the outfit bespoke an intensity and strangeness of affection that Jacey did not feel equal to. Also, it made her uncomfortable about what she had on, cutoffs and T-shirt from her bagging job at the Harris Teeter grocery store.

"What did you get so dressed up for, Leander?"

"You don't like it?"

"No, no, I do like it. It's just, you sort of got a lot going on."

Buttons scanned the ground, unhappily. "My sister Gina did it. I told her I was coming to see you, and she put all this crap on me. I look like a shithead, right?"

Jacey laughed. "No, Leander, you look fine. You look nice. Really nice."

"*You* look nice," said Little Buttons, sauntering to her. He squinted into her face and made her feel shy. He smelled clean. "It's weird to see you."

"Yeah?"

"Yeah. It's weird and great," he said.

Jacey managed not to flinch when he hugged her and gave her a brisk kiss on the cheek. Unreproved, Buttons prolonged the clinch, sighing and gulping in her ear, running his finger along the proud flesh where Jacey's bra strap cut into her back.

"Okay, okay, Leander," said Jacey.

He fell back and went into a fit of feeling his hair. Then he did a queer, vaguely palsied move where he dragged his wrist across his zipper and gave his hips a light twist.

"I'm sorry," he said.

"No, it's cool," said Jacey. "I just wasn't ready to get squeezed like that."

Leander cracked his knuckles.

"So anyway, I think *Jaws* is what we ought to watch, that is if it's *Jaws 1* you've got," Leander said. "I like it when they're on the boat at night."

But Jacey was now unsure if she'd been wise in committing to an afternoon on the sofa with Leander Buttons. An old-time porch swing would have been the thing right then. Before being trapped with him on the couch, she wanted to sit in the open air with Little Buttons, to see in clear light this face that had kissed her in the dark of the orrery.

Jacey balked and squinted at the green cottage across the street as though it had just been built the night before.

"Jacey?"

"What, Leander?"

"Are we going inside?"

"In a minute," said Jacey, with no idea of what she wanted to do.

At that moment, Maya appeared on the front steps. She'd shed her gypsy scarves for a T-shirt, sneakers, and a pair of blue cotton shorts that were not far from underpants. Looking at her cousin, Jacey was suddenly reminded that a theorem for telling whether two right triangles are congruent is "leg-leg."

She was still sore at her cousin over the Charleston phone call, and would be for a long time to come, though she was grateful that Maya didn't smirk or lift an eyebrow at Leander's garb. Maya, the lovely hypocrite, was back to all sweetness and sorority. She said that she was going for a walk. Would Jacey like her to bring back some birch beer or snack cakes from the little store up the road?

Now that Jacey thought of it, a trip to the store seemed like a good idea, the right kind of break-in period she wanted before settling down to *Jaws* and Buttons in the dim light of the den. Jacey suggested they all walk to the store to buy things for "movie salad"—popcorn tossed with Chex mix, M&M's, and plenty of melted butter. Buttons said that he could double Jacey on the Puch. Jacey said no. She had firm views on doubling. She had been pretty good friends with Ricky Murphy, who that past spring had slipped off the back of a scooter and caved his skull in on the curb.

On the walk up Smithfield Road, Maya did not talk of Nureyev, or modeling, or of her own greatness. Instead, she boasted of Jacey's triumphs, her singing voice, and her speed in the fifty-yard dash (Jacey had the surprising fleet-footedness you sometimes find in the plump); how at the girls' camp of their childhood, Jacey had outfoxed a group of Methodists who'd beaten the cousins to the signup sheet for canoes by reminding them that at Judgment the last would be first, and that the meek would inherit the earth. The Methodists had stampeded to be the first to surrender their paddles, and all day the cousins had cruised the lake. Jacey could not help but revel in the praise. Amazing how Maya could make herself nearly impossible to despise for very long.

As it turned out, the store was closed without explanation, and Maya said they should all go to the woods. "Because, check it out," she said, and she pulled from her tiny pants a wizened marijuana jay. What better way to enjoy this day, she pointed out, than to get high among the trees? Leander said what fun it would be to watch *Jaws* behind a buzz. Jacey could not disagree.

The state forest was a realm of oaks and scrub pine blackened from controlled burns, with the new growth already assailed by wisteria and the hairy cursive of poison ivy vines. In search of a toking place, they left the wide gravel lanes where equestrians clopped and took to the secret tracks through the thickets and thorn sward. Jacey and Maya had wandered here often in summers gone by, and Maya led the way through the old hidden trails. How nice it was, thought Jacey, that while three years had passed since they'd been here together, and the girls were not the friends they'd been, some part of Maya still kept a memory of the place.

Leander didn't seem to mind the mud spoiling his Tyrolean loafers, or the rebel strands that had escaped his pomade helmet and swung loose about his face. You could not walk close to him because he was swinging fiercely at the brush with a walking stick he'd found.

But the trek went on longer than it needed to. Maya seemed to have forgotten about the joint and had gone into a pageant of mountain knowledge, showing Jacey and Little Buttons how to identify wild ginger, elderberry, oyster mushrooms, and sassafras. She came across a deer jaw, and wrenched loose the molars and passed them out as brown mementos of the day. Jacey lagged at the rear, now and again losing sight of Leander and Maya in the brush. It annoyed her to hear Buttons plying Maya with his own tidbits on the outdoors—the mythic depth of loblolly taproots, pyrite and arrowhead information, and how you could train a crow to be your pet with patience and crumbs.

Jacey was almost furious when they reached their resting spot—a low bluff with a view of both the main path and the gravy-colored creek at the bottom of the ravine. The waxy leaves of rhododendrons formed a thick barrier from the path. The joggers and equestrians passed by and did not notice them. Nobody saw the teenagers until a youngish man with unruly hair and an old warm-up jacket happened down the trail. He stopped, peering through the bushes. He doffed an imaginary hat and strolled down to the creek. They watched him shed his jacket, shirt, and his boots, and take a seat, Indian-style, on the big island of dun stone in the middle of the stream.

Once the man was past, Maya pulled the joint from her shorts.

"You'll like this stuff," Maya explained to Leander, licking and pinching the paper before she lit it. "Just a nice mild mind high. Not so much a body high."

"Are we gonna smoke it or just fuckin' talk about it?" barked Jacey, who'd had marijuana twice and never felt a thing.

"What's up your butt, Jacey?" Maya asked.

"Nothing. I'm hot. My legs itch." Jacey scratched her calves furiously, and Maya watched.

"Mine get like that, too," Maya said. "Mostly when I haven't gotten exercise in a while."

"I exercise," Jacey snapped. "I swim laps four times a week."

"That's terrific," said Maya. She handed the joint to Leander, along with a thin box of matches.

"A swimming person sweats a gallon of sweat an hour," Leander said. "My brother works at the Community Center pool.

They have to mess with the chemicals constantly to keep up with it. Here, Jacey."

She took the joint and drew a cautious amount of smoke into her cheeks and passed the joint to Maya, who took a long drag and lay back in the shadow of the rhododendrons. Languidly, she put her palms to the sky and went into a spell of practiced breathing. "You know what I love?" she said. "I like the smell, that groovy rotten smell. All these plants that took in the sun and the rainwater out here years ago or whatever; now the leaves and fallen trees are rotting back into the earth, and they're breathing all that energy back out into the air. Literally, that's summer you're smelling, from five, ten, a hundred years ago, all that energy coming back now. I can't explain it. It's sad, but it's beautiful, too."

"I hear you," said Leander.

"You know what else I love?" Maya asked.

"Cheetos?" Jacey offered, trying to rupture the spell of woodland sensuality Maya had begun to weave.

"A Pringle," said Leander Buttons. "A Pringle is a convex paraboloid."

Whatever else it was that Maya loved, she forgot about it when the shirtless fellow down on the creek cranked up a little radio, and suave casino jazz blared dimly through the trees. The music brought Maya to her feet. She felt the air with her palms and swooped her hips around. "Get up, Jacey. Come dance with me."

"I will not."

"Fine, stinker. Leander. Get up. Come here. You don't have a choice."

Leander, nervous and gleeful, allowed Maya to pull him up. She glided around before him, and Leander staggered after her, kind of shadowboxing, his head lolling and looking everywhere, because he couldn't settle on which was the best part of Maya to watch. The next tune started, a waltz. Maya drew Leander to her, squiring him around the bluff. He was grinning like a fool. He got his hands down on the bare gap between Maya's shirt and shorts and left them there.

Jacey could feel the anger coming off her like heat lines on a road. She managed to restrain herself the first time Maya lowered Leander in a competition-grade dip, but the second time, the rage spilled out of her. "All right," she yelled. "You know how to fuckin' dance. We get the goddamned point, Maya. You can sit down now."

Leander and Maya stopped, but they didn't turn each other loose. Maya showed her smooth teeth in a quizzical half smile. "Jesus, what the hell is wrong with you?" she asked. "I asked you to dance and you said no. What do you care?"

"I *don't* care," Jacey said, getting up. "Dance all you want. Or actually, why don't you just go off somewhere and fuck? I mean, there's all kinds of bushes and stuff around here for you all to fuck in."

Maya drew in a sharp, shocked breath and dropped her arms from Leander's shoulders. Leander tittered. Jacey went on. "Yeah, you want to, Leander? She'll totally do it. She's a pretty big slut. See, there's a guy in Charleston she's trying to quit fucking, because of this other guy she's getting ready to fuck, her teacher or somebody, but she can't fuck him yet because he's so goddamned old it's against the law, even though she wants him to."

A collapsed, stunned look came over Maya, as though a piece of crucial rigging had been snipped behind her face. Her mouth hung open wide enough to take a tangerine.

Whatever sound Maya was about to make, Jacey didn't want to hear it. She ran off through the understory, and it was not until she reached the creek that she began to cry. Hot tears rushed out of her. But fearing that Maya and Buttons could see her from their roost, she quickly choked her weeping off and rinsed her sticky face in the creek.

What she wanted most was to go back to the afternoon dark of her mother's house and watch TV and eat Triscuit crackers topped with cheddar cheese and a pickle coin. But to leave the woods, she would have to pass the spot where Maya and Leander were hiding out. She felt she couldn't let them see her heading home and hold on to any dignity, so she wandered the creek, hoping to look distracted and at ease. She walked downstream and upstream again. She pitched rocks into the water. She stroked lichen and squatted for crayfish, which calmed her not at all.

Not far from the bluff, she paused to look at the shirtless man lying out on the stone island. He had his radio going and his eyes closed, as glad in the sun as a cat. She watched him put a green beer bottle to his lips, drain it, and set it in the creek. The bottle bobbed through the eddy and lodged downstream in a wad of beige foam. Then he felt for another in a crowd of bottles clanking in a pool near his hand, opened it, and tipped some of it back, all without opening his eyes. You had to appreciate somebody who all he needed was a hot stone, beer, and a cheap radio to have a good time. Jacey thought she might like to talk to him, just say hello, at least, but he just kept on sunning himself. Minutes went by, and Jacey could feel Maya and Leander's eyes on her, watching her loiter on the bank like a fool.

"Hey!" she called to him.

The man lifted his head to look at her, raising cobbles of

muscle on his stomach. "All right, now," he said with a yawn. He tasted his mouth, blinked, and stacked his fists behind his skull so he wouldn't strain his gut looking at her. "What's happening?"

"You don't have any more of that beer, do you?" Jacey asked.

The man gazed down the path. Then he glanced at the bottles chilling in the creek and scratched at his hair.

"Come on, please," Jacey said. "I'm so thirsty I'm about to die. Give me one. I can pay you for it."

He sat up, looking put-upon, but then he shook his head and chuckled. "I guess," he said. "Come on."

Jacey stepped with care across the algae-sueded rocks that led out to the little island. When she got there, the man had already pulled a beer from the water for her and levered off the cap.

"It's not cold, but it won't burn your mouth," he said. His voice was mild. Jacey took two lusty, gasping pulls on it, and then stared at the bottle with great interest. Shyness warmed her, a heat deeper than the sun's.

"Heineken," she said. "Best beer on the market, if you ask me."

The man didn't say anything but let a mirthful little blast escape from his nose.

"Anyway, I didn't mean to come out here and bug you," Jacey said. She hooked a finger in her pocket and drew out a pair of crumpled bills. "Here. I got two dollars. That enough?"

"Don't sweat it," said the man. "Have a seat, if you like."

Jacey sat, her sturdy pink legs stretched out in front of her, crossed at the ankles, which was how they looked best. She took another deep draw on her beer, and before she could stop it, a terrible wet belch came out of her.

"Gesundheit," the man said, peering back at her with fond gray eyes set deep in merry creases. His blond hair was thinning just a little bit in front, showing a flecked scalp, but you had to look close to see that. A more obvious thing was the condition of his right arm. It was scarred badly at the shoulder. A rumpled welt snaked down the inside of his biceps, tapering almost to his wrist. Black hairs, thick and glossy as stray sutures, punched through the scar here and there. The arm bore three tattoos, all of women, done in surprisingly good taste, none of them posed nude or in an indecent way. The one on his upper arm showed a lady in her middle years, sitting as for a school portrait, her hair parted down the center, wearing a pair of large glasses with half-smoked lenses. A second woman on his forearm was smiling at a little bat-eared dog she cradled in her hands. The third showed a woman dressed in capri pants, fishing in the surf with the sun going down. Jacey had to look at it awhile to notice that in all three pictures, the woman was the same.

"You live near here?" the man asked.

"Pretty close: right off Smithfield Road, which I call Shit-field Road," said Jacey, fast and nervous. "There's nothing going on out here. I wish I lived in town."

"Yeah, town's pretty good if bankers and spear chuckers are your thing," the man said.

He shook a cigarette from a green pack and offered one to Jacey, which she took. She leaned back, smoked, one palm braced on the rock. The bluff was behind her. She hoped Maya and Leander were getting a full load of her, her hair hanging down her back with the sun on it, the beer she'd bravely gotten for herself, and the admirable tobacco smoke rising from her hand.

"I'm Stewart Quick," the man said. "What's your name?"

Jacey told him June, her mother's name.

"Now, I like that," he said. "The girl I probably should have married was named August."

"Why didn't you?"

Quick drew his lips back from his teeth and squinted amiably into the past. "I don't know—fear, stupidity, cash, her old man, and the most god-awful mole you've ever seen, right here," said Quick, pointing at the place where his right nostril joined his cheek. "It was about like a golf ball."

Jacey covered her mouth to hide her braces and laughed into her hand.

"So how old are you, June?" he asked her.

"Guess." She dropped her empty bottle in the creek as she'd seen Quick do.

"Forty-five," he said, handing her another.

"Shut up," said Jacey. "I'm eighteen."

"Now, there's a coincidence," he said. "I'm eighteen, too."

Then he wanted to know things about Jacey: how long she'd lived there on Smithfield Road, what she'd read in school, if she planned to go to college, what she would study there. She told him what felt to her like clever, nimble lies. She figured she'd go to Emory and study premed, but a part of her felt tugged to New York, where a school whose name escaped her had offered her a full ride to study acting and voice.

To everything she said, Stewart Quick would smile and nod and tell her how full of good sense she was, how gifted she must be to have such fine prospects at her feet.

Then he gazed at the rise, at the thick green canopy of oak and gum and pine. "Your buddies still up there?" he asked. "Maybe they'd like to come down and fuck up with us out here on the creek." Jacey didn't like the sound of that. It wounded her to think that Quick didn't feel it, as she did, the special, private atmosphere of just the two of them together on the warm stone.

"Nah," said Jacey. "Those people are stale. I'm not trying to see any more of them today. Hey, let me ask you something, Stewart."

"Yeah, all right."

"Who's that on your arm?" she said. "She's pretty. It's all the same lady, right?"

Quick looked over his tattoos, angling his arm in a pained, ungainly way that caused his lower lip to jut out and shine. "Yeah, my mother. As far as I'm concerned, this is her arm, right here."

"How do you mean, 'hers'?" Jacey pictured that torn and whiskered limb stuck onto that proper-looking woman and she giggled into her bottle.

"I mean I wouldn't have it if it wasn't for her."

"You wouldn't have *you* if it wasn't for her," said Jacey, feeling light and bold with beer.

"If it wasn't for her I'd have lost it, is what I'm saying," said Stewart Quick. The sun slid behind the trees and the light went to bits.

"In the war?" said Jacey.

"Shit, no," said Stewart Quick. "It wasn't in a war; it was in a fuckin' car wash. You want to hear the story?"

Jacey said she did.

"Well, I had this boss. I'm telling you, if you asked me for an asshole, and I gave you that guy, you'd have owed me back some change. Anyway, one day we had a bunch of cars lined up, honking their horns and shit, and this guy's yelling at me to get some clean towels out of the washing machine. Now, I'm not talking an ordinary washing machine. This thing spun about ten times as fast as what you've got at home. So he's going nuts on me, 'Get some towels! Goddammit, get them towels, Stew!' I go over to the machine. I open it up and reach in, only it's not through spinning yet, so what it does, it tears my arm off and dislocates my elbow and crushes up my hand."

"Holy shit, seriously?" said Jacey.

"Yeah, I didn't even know what'd happened, I was in shock so bad. I just walk out into the parking lot in the middle of the afternoon, and it's full of all these people trying to get their Mercedeses and shit cleaned after work. They look up and they see this kid and he's dragging his arm behind him on the concrete like a toy boat, just hanging on by a little thing of skin. Doctors said 'Hell with it, take it off.' But my mom went in there, fuckin' went primal on them, screaming, raising hell. Made them put it back on. They said there wasn't any point. She said, 'I don't give a fuck if it turns black and rots. You sew my son's arm back on. If it dies, we'll cut it off again. But you sew that damn thing on.'"

Quick held up his hand and gave it a remote, appraising look, as though it was a rare object he'd picked up in a store, something he admired but could not afford to buy.

"Kind of a miracle, I guess," said Jacey.

"Pretty cut-rate miracle," he said. "Bone hurts like shit a lot of the time. Plus, I don't have hardly any feeling in my hand."

"That sucks," Jacey said.

Now Quick was touching his thumb to the fingers of his damaged hand, one by one, watching the performance closely, smiling with a kind of mystified amusement. "I don't know. Makes you glad for what you got, I guess. Also, there's something about it, having this part of you you can't feel. Kind of like being two people at once."

"It's not boring, at least," said Jacey. "I think it looks cool, looks tight, those scars and everything."

Quick laughed. He opened another beer and, in handing it to Jacey, he arranged himself beside her, propped on his side, his head close enough to her knee that she could feel his breath drying the sweat on her skin. "How about we swap?" he said. "You take this arm, and I get, I don't know. Maybe I have this leg."

Jacey shied away. "You wouldn't want my big, dumb leg," she said.

"Wrong again," said Quick. "Premium merchandise. Mint condition, except this bit of stuff right here."

Quick put his bad hand around Jacey's calf. He brought his other one to his mouth, sucked for a moment on his thumb, and then used it to rub slow circles over a brown splotch on the inside of Jacey's left leg, just below the knee. She let him do it for a moment. Then she eased her leg from his grasp. It very much alarmed her, the glistening patch Stewart Quick had left there, but she feared it might offend him if she wiped it away. "It's a birthmark," she murmured. When she was a child, her mother had taught Jacey to use the mark to tell her left from right. "When I was little, it was shaped like a fish. It still kind of is."

She had another sip from the bottle, and watched a tiny red beetle struggle through a crevice in the rock. Quick sat up. He took the beer from her, grasped her chin between his forefinger and thumb, and kissed her lightly on the mouth. Then he drew back and watched her with a spreading grin.

"That all right, June?" he said. "Thought I saw you wanting to."

Her lips tingled from Quick's stubble, a complicated sensation. She wondered if her mouth looked different now, disfigured maybe, or possibly altered in a good and glamorous way. She had an urge to touch her lips, but she didn't, afraid that the older man might see it as a rebuke of the unbidden gift.

"Yeah, no," said Jacey. "I was. I mean, I'm glad you did."

Quick let out a satisfied sigh, loud and crisp as a steam leak. "Goddammit, are you kidding me?" he cried. "This is summertime, right here. This is what I'm talking about. This is what a day's supposed to be."

"I know," said Jacey. "I wish there was more of it left."

"Oh, there's plenty," Quick said. "There's lots of it to go."

Quick dipped his hand in the current and daubed the folds of his neck with creek water. "Something just hit me, June."

"What's that?"

"What we need to do to have ourselves the perfect day, we could go up the road to Hidden Lake and take a swim. I just remembered it's Saturday. They'll have a band set up and shit. Got that beer tent going. That's where I need to be."

"Maybe. I don't know," said Jacey. "I've got to meet some people at seven."

Quick looked at his watch. "Well, it's, what, four now, but do what you got to," he said. "I'm just talking about going for an hour or so. That's what I'm going to do."

The red beetle was turning puzzled circles in the shadow of Jacey's ankle. She ushered it onto the narrow canoe of a willow leaf, and set the leaf in the water. It surged through the eddy and out of sight. Then she glanced back at the bluff and saw only leaves. "I guess," said Jacey. "I guess that'd be cool."

Briskly, Stewart Quick donned his shirt and packed away his radio. Then he led Jacey across the creek and down the path, a different one from the path she'd come in on. In fifteen minutes, they reached the trailhead where Quick's car, a two-door Mitsubishi Lancer, was parked. He'd geared it out at some expense—smoked glass, chrome rims, and a large aftermarket windjammer swooping up from the trunk. Quick opened the door for her. Jacey balked. "Just an hour? You swear?" she said.

"No question," said Quick. She got in.

Quick stowed his gear in the backseat. He inserted the key and rolled the windows down but didn't crank the motor. "Hey, come here," he said to Jacey.

"What?" she said.

"Come on over here, June."

She didn't move. Quick leaned over the emergency brake and put his mouth on Jacey's, not as gently as before. He drove his tongue through her teeth and put the palm of his damaged hand against the front of her shorts, moving it with painful force, as though trying to rouse enough sensation for his deaf nerves to feel. Nausea gathered in Jacey's belly. She was sure she was going to vomit or yell, but to humiliate herself in front of the older man seemed an agony at least as bad. Her hand was reaching for the door handle when Quick abruptly turned away and gripped the wheel, and ground the heel of his other hand against his eye, as though something was lodged in there. He mumbled something to himself that Jacey couldn't hear.

For a moment, Jacey thought Quick might open the door and take her back into the woods, but he started the car, pulled onto the road, and patted Jacey's knee in a friendly way. "How we doing there, June? We hanging in?"

"Fine, all right," said Jacey. "Oh, shit, actually, hey, Stewart? I just remembered. Can we turn up here real quick? I need to go by my house for just a second. I want to get my suit."

"You don't need to fool with that," said Stewart Quick.

"Yes, I do. I want to swim. You said we would."

"You can go in what you got on," said Stewart Quick. "It's a laid-back place. People don't care."

"Well, *I* care," Jacey said shrilly. "I'm not going around all day in wet, cold shorts. Now, I need to get my suit."

Quick went silent. She could hear him breathing through his nose. Then he gave a dry, clicking laugh with no amusement in it. "All right, sister," he said. "Whatever you like."

And the car slowed to make the turn.

Her heart beat dizzily. She didn't feel it in her chest so much as on her chin where Quick had grasped it, behind her denim shorts, in her lips, and on her leg where his rough thumb had tried to rub her birthmark off. She had no plan for what to do once she got back to her mother's house, but she figured once she was inside with the door closed, something would come to her.

Quick's Lancer rolled past the Fenhagens', where the twins were out front, wrestling in a plastic pool. They passed the McLures'. Their teenage son was burning the weeds out of the ditch at the edge of their lawn. In the afternoon sun, the flames were invisible, just a band of jellied air.

"It's just here," said Jacey. They rounded the curve. Quick pulled up to the house. Jacey's father's silver Buick was in the driveway, three hours early, and when she saw it, what she did not feel was relief.

"Whoa," said Stewart Quick. "Who's this guy?"

Her father was out there on the lawn, pulling dead petals from the rosebushes he'd planted there many years before. At the sound of Quick's tires on the gravel, before he could even make out his daughter behind the tinted glass of the shotgun window, he turned and gave a clumsy wave, the brown petals spilling from his hand.

At the sight of her father, the fear went out of Jacey, and cold mortification took its place. There he stood, not yet forty, bald as an apple, and beaming out an uncomprehending fat-boy's smile. His face, swollen with a recent sunburn, glowed against the green dark of the rosebushes at his back. He wore the cheap rubber sandals Jacey hated, and a black T-shirt airbrushed with the heads of howling wolves, whose smaller twin lay at the bottom of Jacey's closet with the price tag still attached. Exhausted gray socks collapsed around his thick ankles, which rose to the familiar legs Jacey herself was afflicted with, bowed and trunk-like things a lifetime of exercise would never much improve. Her humiliation was sudden and solid and without thought or reason. But the wordless, exposed sensation overwhelming her was that her father wasn't quite a person, not really, but a private part of her, a curse of pinkness and squatness and cureless vulnerability that was Jacey's right alone to keep hidden from the world. Whatever desirable thing Stewart Quick had seen in her, she knew it couldn't survive the association with the stolid smiler walking toward her over the Bermuda grass.

Jacey opened the door. "You coming back?" asked Quick, his voice a little urgent.

She didn't answer. "There she is," her father said. "Where you been, Jace? I've been waiting here an hour."

"Well, what the hell for?" hissed Jacey. "Seven's what you said."

"Oh," said her father. "I tried to call. I got off early. I just thought before we grabbed dinner we'd go out to Emerald Pointe."

Her father looked beyond her to the crass yellow bird of Stewart Quick's idling Mitsubishi.

"Who's that, Jacey? Who're you with?"

Behind her a car door opened, and Quick called out her mother's name. Jacey jogged past her father to the house. She had to dodge Leander's moped to reach the brick path. Probably, they'd be back here any second, he and Maya, to swell the day's festival of shame to its maximum pitch. Jacey ran through the door, up the carpeted stairs to her bedroom, to discover some small good news. The cat, after many hours of imprisonment, had finally gotten around to the pigeon hatchling on Jacey's bed, though its appetite had given out with a pink foot and a bruised triangle of bald wing remaining on the quilt. When

Jacey came panting through the door, the cat leaped from the windowsill where it had been napping, and bounded to the bed. It slouched around the leavings of the bird, watching Jacey with wrathful eyes. But after a while, the cat relaxed and, satisfied that Jacey posed no threat, took up the last of its meal.

ON THE SHOW

Now it's dark. The sun has slipped behind the orange groves, disclosing the garbled rainbow of the carnival rides. The blaring reds of the Devil's Choir and the blue-white of the Giant Wheel and the strobing greens of the Orbiter and the chasing yellow and purple of the Chaises Volantes mingle and the sky glows hyena brown. Panic takes hold among the egrets in the drainage canal. They flee for the live-oak tree that surveils the hay-bale corral of the World's Smallest Horse. For a time, the tree moves with a white restlessness of egrets stowing and unstowing their overlong wings.

Shadow falls across the Crab Rangoon stand. A Florida anole, cocked on the shoulder of the propane tank beside the service window, slips down the tank's enamel face into a crescent of deep rust. Against the lizard's belly, the rust's soothing friction offers an illusion of heat, and the lizard's hide goes from the color of a new leaf to the color of a dead one.

The lizard's movement catches the eye of Henry Lemons, seven years old, who reaches for it, curling his fingers so that they form a small damp hollow around the animal.

"What'd you get?" asks Randy Cloatch, age ten, who stands

beside him. The two boys just met tonight. Jim Lemons, Henry's father, has come to the fair on a blind date with Sheila Cloatch, Randy's mother. Jim Lemons is the manager of a market research firm in Norton Beach, whose city limits lie two miles down the road. Sheila's sister, Destiny Cloatch, works in the call center, and she arranged the date.

Their evening together is going very well—too well for Henry and Randy, who for forty minutes have been loitering on the midway, watching the couple go around and around way up there on the Giant Wheel. They can see Randy's mother's hair, so blond it shines white, gusting around the yellow baseball cap Jim Lemons wears to hide a bald place on his scalp.

Henry holds the lizard against his chest. "Nothing. Just a little lizard."

"Yeah? Chameleon? What color?" Randy wants to know. "Give him here."

Henry dilates the careful prison of his fist. What a nice lizard it is. Look at how his lipless mouth creases upward at the ends in a wise little smile, as though pleased to be in Henry's grasp. His ribs pulse quick and soft against the dirty whorls of Henry's thumb. The only sign of alarm the lizard gives is the color leaching through his hide, a color a casual eye might call green. But Henry Lemons, who has brought the lizard within two inches of his eye, can see that the lizard's skin is no single hue but is in fact a mosaic of tiny yellow and blue discs.

"It's no color," he tells Randy.

"Bullshit, give him here," Randy says, swatting after Henry's clutched fist.

"Bull-true, you fat shit. Get away. He's mine."

Randy Cloatch flushes. At one hundred and seventy pounds, Randy is the fattest ten-year-old at the Indian River County

Fair, and he is probably the fattest ten-year-old in Indian River County as well. His arms are like bowling pins. His breasts swing when he walks. Randy wears a heavy blue cast on his left leg. Two weeks earlier, he was hammering the coin plunger on a newspaper machine when the machine fell over and cracked the bone just below his dimpled knee.

Randy is used to being jibed about his weight, though it seems unfair that Henry should make fun of him now, while he is wearing his cast. What makes the insult even worse is that Henry Lemons is as outlandishly beautiful as Randy Cloatch is obese. Henry is slender, with eyes as dark and glassy as a mare's. His loveliness makes grown men and women fall silent. Randy Cloatch wants to hit Henry Lemons, but Henry's beauty emanates a costly sort of power that stalls his hand. It is the same hesitation that seizes him when he is throwing stones at cars passing on the four-lane road beside his mother's house and an obviously new or expensive one comes along.

"Hey, I'll give you two tickets for him," says Randy Cloatch, hoping to banish the insult by ignoring it.

Henry points out that you can't buy anything with two tickets. Even a ride on the trudging Shetlands in the pony rotary costs three. He also explains that the tickets in Randy's damp hand are technically Henry's anyway, seeing how Randy wouldn't have any tickets at all if Henry's dad hadn't cashed in a pair of fifty-dollar bills and given tickets to both Randy and his mother.

Randy grabs the smaller boy's wrist, groping for Henry's fist, hoping to force him to crush the lizard. Henry lets out a noise so shrill that Randy lets go of his arm, and Henry sprints off down the midway, past the Teacup and the screaming ruby blur of the Fireball, the Gorilla Girl Alive!, and the Pirate. He ducks down an alley between the Nickel Extreme and the Ghost Train, through a colonnade of portable toilets that the carnival workers use. He finds himself in the trailer lot, where the light suddenly stops, except for the orange droplets on the running boards of idle trucks, dim in the diesel smog.

Henry waits in the dark, leaning against a truck grille stuccoed over with crisp insects, and watches the Giant Wheel turn. He cannot see his father, but he knows he is on that slowly turning wheel. He decides he'll watch the wheel revolve forty times, a number Henry feels close to, because that's how old his father is. He watches it turn eighteen times, loses count, and starts again. The lizard scratches at his palm. He has counted back up to twenty-two, when he notices a man watching him from the pillar of darkness between the outhouses. When he sees Henry notice him, the man walks over to the boy. Henry is afraid that the man might be the owner of the truck he is leaning against, or that he's come to catch Henry out for straying into an area into which not even the orange tickets coiled in his pocket permit him to go.

When the man asks Henry what he's up to here, Henry tells him about how Randy Cloatch is after him. The man nods as though he's familiar with Randy Cloatch, as though through some trick of time he also suffered at Randy's hand when he was small. The man says that Randy won't find them back here, and if he does, the man has a way of taking care of it. Henry grins, wishing Randy *would* step back in here and see what he would get. The man lights a cigarette. He looks back toward the fair with concern in his face. He tells Henry, on second thought, maybe they ought to hide out awhile, just until the coast is clear. Henry, worried now, asks the man if he is sure. The man says yes, that he knows a place, and he leads Henry into the privy at the end of the row, his steady hand, warm and assuring as a water bottle, pressing between the boy's shoulder blades.

The privy is yellow plastic, brand name Honeypot. The man pulls shut the Honeypot's door.

"Here we go—safe," the man says, and slides the black tab across the jamb. The plastic door is queered with heat and age. A canted square of brown light seeps through the doorway. In the half light, Henry can make out the man's belt buckle, a silver disc with a circle of blue stone in its center.

The lizard leaps from Henry's open hand and slips beneath the door. Once outside, it settles in a pocket in the sand where a trace of the sun's heat lingers.

Warm, damp nights like this one are unpleasant for Leon Delaney, the foreman on the Pirate. Leon is a giant, with a head like a fire hydrant and palms the size of dinner plates. The night's heat stokes the psoriasis reddening his arms, and he sits in the doghouse, rasping at his rash with a shingle-thick nail so that the sloughings fall on the black metal of the ride's control panel. Leon is sixty-three, and because he's had three heart attacks, he is sober except for beer. For nostalgia's sake, he pauses now and again to mound the dead skin into a line and guesses at its cash value if the skin were good cocaine.

A young man named Jeff Park stands at the railing, studying a hand-lettered sign reading "Ride Jock Needed."

Leon doesn't like the look of Jeff Park, his boat shoes, or the lobe of hair that hangs over one of his eyes. Leon prefers to hire broke men fleeing bench warrants to sun-kissed beach slouchers. The lieutenant on the pirate ship is more Leon's kind of hire, a wizened fellow named Ellis who smiles and schemes and doesn't leave Leon wondering for an instant what kind of man he is. Even now, Ellis is supposed to be mopping some puke off the floor of the ride, but he uses the occasion of Jeff's arrival to lay aside his mop and have his dinner—a can of beef soup he tips cold into his mouth. But Leon's crew is short as of last night, when the third hand took a piss break and didn't come back. He needs another man before they take the ride apart when the show packs up two days from now.

"Hey, friend, you looking for a job?" The giant's voice sounds as though it runs on gasoline.

"Yeah, guess so," Jeff says. "What's it pay?"

The giant looks him over. His thumb and forefinger could go twice around Jeff's upper arm. "You like hard work? You into lifting shit?"

"I'm all right with it. And what's the pay, again?"

"Buck-eighty a week, seven days." He watches to see whether Jeff flinches at this felonious wage.

"That'll work," says Jeff, by which Leon understands that the young man is in a bad pinch. He should have led with $150.

"Need something to eat?"

The young man nods.

The giant reaches into his pocket and brings out a ten-dollar bill.

Jeff looks at the money. "Seriously?"

"It comes back to me on Friday." Leon then lists the other sums that will come out of his pay: thirty dollars for a hat and shirt, fifteen for an ID, forty dollars per week for a bunk on the carnival train. Jeff Park stands blinking. He has been on the show for fifty seconds and he already owes the giant eighty-five dollars.

Ellis tosses his cigarette away and jogs down from the upper deck to meet the new man. He is a tall fellow, in his early thirties, but he has a face like a paper bag smoothed flat by a dirty palm.

"Your name's what, now?" Ellis asks.

"Parts," Leon answers for him.

"No," says Jeff. "Park. No *s*. With a *k*."

"Like 'going to the park,'" says Ellis.

"Yeah," says Jeff.

"That's good, I like that," says Ellis.

"A hole is better than some of the Parks," roars Leon from the doghouse, and his laughter scatters the hoarded skin.

By the time they've had enough of the Giant Wheel, Sheila Cloatch thinks she might be a little bit in love with Jim Lemons. They kissed a couple of times up there, and in the high quiet over the bright grid of the fair, it seemed to matter more somehow, to count. He was careful with her body, not like her ex-husband, who would grab at her like he was trying clutch his way to a place where he'd never have to touch a woman again. Jim Lemons is different. She had to put his hand up her skirt because he wouldn't do it on his own. She likes his shyness, his glasses, and his arms, which have muscles but not much hair. She'd like to invite him back to her apartment, to put the boys in front of the Nintendo and sit out on her little concrete balcony, drinking the expensive blue cognac liqueur she'd laid in. It won't give you any hangover if you mix it with Gatorade.

Sheila's son, Randy, is waiting alone by the platform, picking at his cast. His mother gets it out of him that he and Henry Lemons had an argument. "Goddammit, you're ten. He's seven. You's supposed to look out for him."

"But, Mom, he called me a shit," pleads Randy Cloatch.

"I'll call you worse than that," she hisses. "Seven years old and you ran him off."

Twenty minutes later, Jim Lemons finds his son at the head of the midway, watching a man in a bow tie demonstrate the mystical absorbency of a square of chamois cloth. Henry doesn't say much about what happened to him in the privy, but he says enough. Jim isn't sure about the story. In his heart, he believes Henry is a dishonest boy, that his beauty has made him as vindictive and conniving as a movie star. Little fistfuls of coins go missing from Jim's change jar when Henry comes over. On their last visit, Henry claimed a rattlesnake wagged its tail at him through the sink drain and he begged to go back to his mother's. He wouldn't give up the lie all weekend, even when Jim spanked him for it. Jim would suspect the boy of lying now, of deliberately trying to ruin his date. But Henry is missing his underwear and one of his shoes, which gives the story a bad ring of truth.

Jim brings Henry to a police officer staffing a booth devoted to DUI awareness. More police arrive. A patrolman explains to Jim Lemons that he will have to take him and his son to the police station in town to log his statement and conduct an exam. Henry isn't crying, or even close to it, but the tears are coming out of Sheila Cloatch like she's auditioning for something. Mascara soot runs down her neck. She gives Jim a long, fierce hug. Her bleached hair gives off a reek of scorched plastic, and her breath is sharp from the gin they had with frozen lemonade on the Giant Wheel.

"I'll ride with you to the station, Jim," she says. "I'll be there with you. I want to."

What Jim wants Sheila to do is leave before the officers notice how drunk she is. "I don't think that'll be necessary," says Jim, using his office voice. He leaves her and goes to the waiting patrolman, who insists that Jim and Henry ride with him in the cruiser. Jim Lemons understands that the policeman is suggesting that he might have reason to tamper with the evidence left on his son, but he feels so waterlogged by the night's events that he doesn't take offense.

The cruiser rolls out of the Midway, through the parking lot, to the county road where the stars get the sky back from the fair.

"How we doing, chief?" Jim Lemons asks Henry, who is humming the theme song from a television show.

"Fine," says Henry in a flat voice that refuses Jim the comfort of providing comfort.

Jim Lemons tries not to think about what Henry might have experienced in the portajohn. Instead, he concentrates his worry on the phone call he should already have made to his ex-wife. The split wasn't friendly. She spent a lot of lawyer money to make sure Jim doesn't get to see Henry more than two days a month. When he let Henry watch *Harry Potter*, she asked the parenting coordinator to cut his time in half on grounds of parental irresponsibility. Jim Lemons has a hunch that it could be months, maybe years, before he sees his son again. This is how he'll have to remember Henry for a good long time: one shoe on, eyes dull as nickels.

He scratches his neck. It itches, the little red dent where Sheila Cloatch's big earring pressed against him for a while.

Here is how Jeff Park wound up on the show:

At the age of fifty-eight, Jeff's mother met a man on the computer and moved to his house in Melbourne, Florida, which was large with a view of the beach. Jeff was in Phoenix, taking a break from school, and his mother flew him out to spend a week or two. It turned out to be just his sort of life in Melbourne—a little three-room mini apartment to himself, and down on the strip, five different bars where you had women going around in bathing suits. In the backyard, his mother's new husband had grown a miraculous tree, a lemon trunk grafted with orange, tangerine, satsuma, kumquat, and grapefruit limbs, each bearing its own vivid fruit. Every morning, Jeff would go out and fill his arms, and squeeze himself a pitcher of juice, thick and sun-hot. That house was good for his mother, too. The swimming pool trimmed fifteen pounds off of her. She didn't seem to have moods anymore, and she didn't fly off the handle when Jeff beat her in the cribbage games they played most afternoons. Jeff's visit lasted four months, and he figured he'd let it go on four months more, at least.

His mother's husband, David, was a quiet man without much to say to Jeff Park. A retired optometrist pushing seventy, he spent his days in the backyard greenhouse, where he grew tournament peonies, their blossoms as red and heavy as beef hearts. Days would go by and the two men wouldn't trade a single word. But one morning last week, he came to Jeff's room with something to say. "Jeffrey, there's a favor you can do for me." He placed a green tub of Turtle Wax on his bedside table. So Jeff spent three angry hours squatting in the sun on the white concrete of the driveway, waxing the old man's Volvo and the Audi wagon he'd given Jeff's mother to drive.

Then today, while Jeff was on the glider in the sunroom, reading a magazine, David pulled up in a Chevy Suburban and presented Jeff with another tub of Turtle Wax. The Suburban, he explained, belonged to a gentleman in his barbershop quartet whose wrists were bad.

"You want me to wax your *buddy's* truck?" Jeff asked.

"That's correct," the old man said.

Jeff laughed and went back to his magazine. He said, "That's a good one," and the old man slapped him hard on the face. Then a leggy, grunting scramble happened on the brick floor of the sunroom. Spit and four months of stored hate poured out of the gray gentleman. Jeff put him on his back and got the old man's stringy biceps under his knees. He didn't want to hit him, hoping in a minute or two the fever would leave his step-father, but he stayed red and foaming, trying to thrash free. Jeff's mother went out of the house to wail by the pool. Jeff told the old man he was going to get off of him and leave the house for good. David closed his eyes and nodded. Then, when Jeff took his knees off of his stepfather's arms, the old man did a move where he tried to bite Jeff on his balls. He missed, how-ever, and clamped his teeth on Jeff's bare inner thigh where his shorts had hiked up. He broke the skin. At that point, Jeff did find it in his heart to punch the old man many times on the hinge of his jaw. When it was over, dark blood was pooling in his stepfather's ear, and Jeff had a hole in his thigh. Jeff Park got up and stuffed some clothes into a bag. Then he ran past his mother and out through the peony garden, where the sprinklers were coming on.

A detective stops by the Pirate, wanting to know where Leon and Jeff Park were at six fifteen that evening. Leon says to the cop that he was sitting right here on his stool with about a hun-dred motherfuckers watching him. Jeff Park says that he was walking up from Melbourne on the shoulder of Route 1. "That," says the detective with a chuckle, "isn't one of the seven alibis of highly effective people."

"For what? What happened?" Jeff Park asks.

"Anyway," the detective says. "We'll get it all straightened out when we come back and get a sample of you-all's blood and hair." He copies down the information from Jeff's driver's license and then he goes to buy an elephant ear.

When the cop is gone, Ellis crawls out of the engine well.

"Fuck were you?" Leon asks.

"Shimming blocks," Ellis says.

Leon tells the story of the cop and the DNA samples, and Ellis spits in the dirt. "That right there's a classic case of some horseshit," he says. "They can't take your hair without a court order."

"They can take mine," Jeff Park says. "I didn't do anything."

Ellis smiles. "Yeah, but even if you did."

At the pirate ship, a line of riders grows at the entry corral, among them Sheila Cloatch and her wide son. Sheila's face is powdered white, and her hair is white, and she wears white jeans and a white halter top. With his blue cast, orange shirt, pink face, and black hair, it's as though Randy somehow siphoned the color from his mom.

"I don't care about this gay-rod boat," Randy says. "I want to go home."

"That works out good. We only got enough tickets for one." Sheila's in a bitter mood. Her heart goes out to Jim Lemons. She's prayed three times already for Jim and his son, yet she can't help but think what a waste it is that he left in the patrol car with at least forty dollars' worth of ride tickets in his pocket.

She hands her last three tickets to Jeff Park, who says, "I'm sorry. It's four to get on."

"You go on, ma'am," Ellis says, waving her three tickets away. Sheila thanks them and takes a seat.

"I'm the king of that shit," Ellis says.

"What?" asks Jeff Park.

"If it's a double-breasted split-tail, letting 'em on for free. It works. Man, I've had a avalanche of pussy. Only goddamn fringe benefit you get out here."

The engines engage. The men stand together on the deck's upper tier, watching the fan of Sheila Cloatch's hair blurring with the swing of the ship.

"Blond to the bone," says Ellis. "I'd eat her whole damn *child* just to taste the thing he squeezed out of."

Word gets around that the police are looking for a man who took a child into a toilet, which, at the pirate ship, inspires talk of crime and punishment.

"Hey, Parts," the giant barks at the new man. "What's the best state to get sent up on a capital beef?" Jeff Park doesn't know.

The answer is Delaware. "In Delaware you get a choice of how they kill you, which means you can still choose hanging."

"So what?" says Jeff.

"Here's what. If they miss on the first shot—leave you paralyzed, whatever—they have to turn you loose. That's in the Bill of Rights. Now, I've never heard of anyone making it through lethal injection, but with hanging you've got a chance. You'd be in funny shape, but you got that sporting chance."

The citizens are running out of things to look at in this town. They had a handsome five-story condo skyscraper, but a sinkhole opened under it. A major league baseball team used to spring-train here, but it left years ago for the dry air of Santa Fe.

All that's left to gaze on are the citrus orchards and the green void of the sea.

How hungry the fairgoers' eyes are tonight! Everything amazes them. When Ellis climbs into the high steel of the Pirate to change a lightbulb, leaning into the vertex of the trusses sixty feet up, his sneakers just barely lipping the bolt heads he's standing on, a crowd gathers to yell, "Don't slip!" When a teenage boy spies Leon's tattoos—two twisted pairs of fives and a blurry swastika where the tattooer finally got the angles right—the Pirate becomes temporarily popular with teens who line up to titillate themselves with glimpses of the giant's wicked hand.

The ride jocks and concessionaires like to look at Gary, the man who runs the Zipper, a chain-saw-shaped ellipse with spinning cars instead of teeth. When the ride is running, Gary bobs and dodges beneath the Zipper, collecting the pocket change and cigarettes that rain down from the cars. The cars hurtle dangerously close, but Gary knows the interval of safety, and how the air piles up when a car is coming close. He moves with a weird and swooning grace, vaguely Oriental, a feinting dream of wind. If Gary were not lightly retarded, Leon says he could make good money on a stage in Las Vegas, but he is here, beloved and famous among the people on the show.

A rain comes. The crowd shrinks into little drifts beneath booth awnings and then disappears. Jeff Park somersaults a quarter back and forth across his knuckles. Ellis finds the quarter stunt amazing, and insists that Jeff teach it to him.

The giant does not like the shine that Ellis is taking to the new man. Leon knows it won't be long before he's too old for the days of heavy steel work that come every two weeks when the show packs up. His foremanship is at risk, and the alliance between the younger men bodes mutiny.

"Want to see *my* magic trick?" Leon says to Jeff Park.

"Yeah, all right."

Leon takes the cigarette from his mouth and taps a long gray caterpillar of ash onto Jeff Park's shoulder.

"Presto change-o, you're an ashtray."

A woman stands at the gate of the pirate ship, staring at nothing. "Come on, lady," Ellis howls at her. "Come and be a buccaneer."

The woman's face is as blank and guileless as a peeled apple. "What type of ride is this?" she asks Jeff Park, who now understands she is blind.

"It's a boat," he says. "You sit on it and it swings."

"Does it go upside down?"

"No, but it goes really fast."

"But not upside down?"

"No."

"Okay, then. I want to ride."

She clasps Jeff's hand, holding him close as a lover as they make their way up the platform. With each step, her foot hovers in the air, searching for treacheries in the ground beneath her. Jeff holds on to the thick flesh of her waist and eases her onto the bench.

The ride begins, and Jeff watches the blind woman, ready to give word to stop the boat if she begins to panic, but she doesn't. The man beside her roars in terror when the boat goes weightless at the limit of its swing. But the blind woman smiles as though she's just recalled the answer to a question that had been worrying her for a long time. The ride ends, and Jeff goes to her and helps her down the platform. She is warm against him and cannot stop laughing. "Thank you, thanks very much," she says, and Jeff Park feels glad to have found work on the Pirate, a machine that draws joy out of people as simply as a derrick draws oil from dirt.

When the crowds take off, and the lights go out at once, the people on the show board the bus that carries them to the carnival train. The windows are cataracted with blue grime. The bus has no seats. The destination slot above the windshield reads "Palm Beach Tour."

Ellis has a spare bunk in his berth on the train, left vacant by the Pirate crew member who wandered off the day before. Jeff balks, and Ellis says, "Or go bunk with the Mexicans. But just so you know, they'll steal the stink off shit."

Jeff takes Ellis's spare bunk. The air in the berth is humid and rotten. But Jeff is so tired that the promise of sleep is every bit as voluptuous to him as sex or food. He crawls onto the top bunk and lays his cheek against the rubber mattress, which shows brown spangles of old drool.

Presently, the bed creaks and quakes while Ellis brusquely adores himself in the bunk below. When Ellis is finished, he's in the mood for talk.

"Think you'll stick around awhile, Park?" he asks Jeff.

"Guess so," says Jeff. "You stand there and they pay you for it."

"Talk to me when we have to break that fucker down." Ellis's hand appears in the gap between Jeff's mattress and the wall. One of his fingers is blue to the second knuckle. "That cocksucker Leon dropped a beam on it, and he laughed about it. Thought I lost the damn thing. If he killed you or me, I don't think he'd even look on that as being a bad day."

Jeff says he'll look out.

"I don't mean no disrespect, but you don't know what to look out for. *I'll* look out for you. I'll take care of the high-steel shit, for the next stop or two, anyway, and you help me out when you can. Nobody survives out here by theirself. You need a partner on the show."

"Right on," says Jeff. He thinks of the eighty-five dollars he owes the giant, and he gets a bad feeling that he owes Ellis something now.

A workday on the show lasts sixteen hours, so at night the carnival train echoes and howls with people trying to fit in some living between midnight and dawn.

At 2:20 a.m. by Jeff Park's watch, someone kicks open the door of his neighbor's berth. "What the fuck are you doing?" a man's voice cries.

There is no answer, just a crash. Jeff feels the tin wall buckle under his feet.

At 4:10 a.m., in the berth at Jeff's head, a woman says, "I mean, you ate my fucking heart, Ron. De*voured* it, like a buzzard, straight out of my chest." There is a gagging back of tears. "Oh, God, Ron, why do I love you so goddamned much? Only thing I love more than you is my kids. No, fuck that. I love you more than my kids."

"Would you shut up, Suzanne? You're embarrassing me."

The sobbing breaks off, and Suzanne says, "You're embarrassing yourself."

At ten at the fairgrounds, all the carnival workers line up at the top of the midway for a free lunch, courtesy of the county fire-fighters, who didn't know what else to do with eighty pounds of barbecued chicken left over from their booth the night before. The breasts are in the firehouse freezer. It is a dark-meat-only lunch, one leg and one thigh. At the end of the buffet stands the county detective. Before a firefighter's wife hands out dessert, a slice of pecan log, the detective asks the male workers to lift their shirtfronts, checking belt buckles. Then he snaps their portraits to show to Henry Lemons later in the day.

Jeff Park eats his chicken leg alone in the agriculture pavilion, which is full of oat smells and the agreeable bellyaching of competition cattle.

He visits with the rabbits in their cages, and pokes his finger into an enclosure that holds a large gray hare. The hare flexes the pink cleft of his nose at Jeff's finger and then nips it hard. When Jeff pulls his finger back, a button of blood is growing on his fingertip. "I am a California Dutch to be used in the meat competition," reads a sign on the cage.

Jeff hears the clatter of hose water in the far end of the pavilion. A boy of fourteen or so stands beside a lustrous black steer, holding a blue bucket full of suds. He empties the bucket along the animal's back and soapy water runs down in pale drips like the icing on a Bundt cake. He hoses the steer down, and then pulls a Scotch comb in long parentheses down the steer's ribs, ushering peels of water into the sawdust. In the comb's wake, the steer's coat gleams like fresh tar.

Only when the boy has combed out one side of the steer does he turn and notice Jeff. The boy's name is Chad. He's clean and so full of health, and Jeff is drawn to him. "Pretty bull," says Jeff.

"Steer," says Chad.

"What's the difference?"

"A steer's where you take his balls. Want to buy him?"

"How much?" says Jeff.

"I'll be pissed if he goes for less than twelve hundred."

"You sell him for meat?"

"Beef project, yeah."

"Seems weird to go through the hassle of making him look so good if he's just going to get killed for beef."

"You end up meat someday, but you still comb your hair in the morning," he says. "Or ought to."

The boy picks up his bucket and disappears behind the animal's spine.

Jeff Park sits on a hay bale by the petting zoo, where he watches a goose chase a pygmy hog. He has not been sitting there long when he notices that Ellis is standing on the far side of the pen, looking at him. Ellis leans down to scratch the hog's nose, and the hog grunts appreciatively.

"I skinned a hog one time, when I was a kid in Kentucky," he says, and eases himself down on a bench. "Razorback. Blocked it out myself—hams, shoulders, side meat, all that stuff. Deer, squirrel. I can skin anything, just about." He shakes his head. "Nobody here knows that. Nobody here don't know nothing about me."

Jeff Park says he feels the same way.

Ellis smiles. "You're like me. You're quiet. You keep to yourself. That's good."

"I guess."

Ellis pats the bench beside him. "Come over here," he says.

Jeff walks over but doesn't take a seat. "You look like you're down about something. Look like you got something on your mind."

"Nothing much," Jeff says. "Kind of tired, I guess."

"Uh-uh," Ellis says, grinning. "You can't lie to me. It's more than that. I can tell."

The young cattleman ambles past, leading his gleaming steer. Ellis turns. He watches the boy with what strikes Jeff Park as disconcerting intensity, his head bobbing slightly to take in the motion of the young man's gait, as though the event must be recorded in a perfect and durable way. This image comes to Jeff Park's mind: Ellis asquat in the portable toilet with the schoolchild. Jeff doesn't recall seeing him in line for the chicken, the photo, and the pecan log. He considers mentioning Ellis to the detective. But, unsure of how to phrase his inkling in a way that wouldn't sound hysterical or invite suspicion on himself, Jeff abandons the idea and goes back to the Pirate Ship.

In the afternoon, the crowds slacken. Leon sits in the doghouse, bawling out a balladry of lies:

"They said I had a cancer on my shoulder blade, and it'd cost ten grand to fix it. Instead, I drank some rye, and my man got in there with a box knife. He cut out a mess of these little purple marbles, and I've been fine ever since.

"You ever see that movie with Steve Martin, happens at the circus? Had me a little part in it. Well, one day he comes up to me—Steve Martin—tells me to go get him a root beer, and fast or he'd get me canned. Know what I did? Turned right around and poled the son of a bitch."

Ellis laughs, and Jeff sits on the upper deck, his back turned to the men. He's thinking of his bedroom in Melbourne. The wound pulses in his thigh, and he contemplates the famous microbial vileness of the human mouth.

"Park's sulled up on us, Leon," Ellis says to the giant. "I don't think he likes us anymore."

"I just don't feel like talking, Ellis," Jeff says. "That a problem?"

"Shit, yeah, it's a problem. You make the time go slow."

Ellis fetches a lightbulb from a carton in the doghouse, and points out a dud in the bulbs that ring the leering pirate's head hanging high above the ship.

"Here you go, Park, get up there," Ellis says, handing Jeff the bulb.

Park gazes at the climb, fifty feet up an extension ladder, lashed to the back of a support stanchion with nylon rope frayed to needles. His legs feel watery to look at it.

"I thought—I thought you said you'd do the high work, Ellis," says Jeff Park.

Ellis sucks a tooth. "I changed my mind."

Jeff scales the stanchion with the lightbulb in his mouth. The ladder is missing rungs, and his arms tremble as he climbs. He has nearly reached the top when a sudden wind rocks the ladder. "Oh," Jeff cannot help but say. The lightbulb drifts from his lips and shatters on the deck.

"Three dollars," the giant calls up to him. "Them shits don't grow on trees."

On a weeknight, you can spend ten dollars on a special yellow pass and have as many rides as you want. A fifteen-year-old girl boards the Pirate nine times in a row. It's hot out, but she's sweating in a fuzzy orange sweater. She's perpetually sucking the phosphorescent candy they sell at the fair. Each time

Jeff Park tugs her lap bar to be sure it's locked down tight, he steals a glimpse of the pale green light glimmering behind her teeth, a light of both desolation and comfort, the light of a lone cottage window on an empty street. He thinks it's there for him.

"I'm Katie," she tells him on her tenth ride. "I've seen you so many times, I thought I ought to introduce myself."

He says his name. "I don't know how you keep riding this thing. I'd probably puke if I rode it once."

"You stand out here all night, and you never rode it?"

"No," says Jeff.

She bobbles the light on her tongue. "That's the most retarded thing I've ever heard all day. Hey, can you do me a favor?"

"What kind?"

"Can you make it go extra long this time?"

"I'll see what I can do." The ride starts up. As the boat swings, Katie watches him, and he watches the blur in her green summer mouth.

When the swinging stops, she leaves to watch the hatchet juggler at the Village of Yesteryear, but twenty minutes later, she comes back.

"Remember me?" she says to Jeff, and by way of greeting slips her fingers into his hand.

"Nope," he says, grinning.

"Oh, shut up. You do, too."

He has time to chat with her while the benches fill up.

"Do you know any secrets?" she asks him.

"Yes."

"Fair stuff, I mean. Like, can you show me how to win at the games?"

"Don't mess with them in the first place."

"Hey, don't be stale. They don't show you the tricks?"

"Yeah, but I can't tell you."

"Why not?"

"I don't know. They'd feed me to the mermaids." He gestures across the midway at the Weeki Wachee Girls, three pretty ladies in bikini tops and fishtails, writhing together in a Plexiglas crate of luminous water.

"Sounds like a thrill for you."

When the boat stops, the girl calls him over.

"Hey," she says to Jeff. "Do they ever let you off of here, or do you have to stand on this thing all night?"

"I get a half hour at nine. What's up?"

She shrugs. "I don't know. You want to maybe kick it for a while? You could win me some crap."

"Sure," Jeff says.

"How about over there, at that thing where you toss the dimes?"

"All right."

"Go on, now. Get this thing moving. Get me as high as you can."

Night falls, and an envelope arrives for Gary, the dancing Zipper man. He sees it float down through the rushing darkness, a square of folded cellophane. When the ride is over, he goes into the doghouse and opens the letter, which to Gary's glad surprise contains a minor turd of brown heroin. On the floor of the doghouse, he finds a piece of tinfoil, on one side smeared with the leavings from a chili dog, and folds it into a square. Angling the foil in a shallow ramp, he daubs the dope to the top of the grade and holds his lighter under it. As the turd melts and slides, it leaves a smoking stain behind it. Gary sucks the smoke with clasping lips, taking in a flavor of vinegar and seasoned beef.

The passengers are waiting. He goes out and locks them in the cars. Then he starts the engine and slips under the ride to dance for more falling gifts. But now Gary's awareness of spinning, swooping things swells beyond the simple motion of the Zipper to take in the whole of the tumbling midway, and beneath all that the vaster, subtler revolutions of the very planet. He is gone in communion with some far-off turning thing when he loses the rhythm of the Zipper, fails to sense the wind against his skin. The angle-iron prow of a barreling car smacks him on the back bulge of his skull. The car carries him for a moment, and then drops him in the sand.

Jeff Park visits the cinder-block toilet bunker up by the band shell. In the square of dented tin serving as a mirror, he sees an unfamiliar face looking back at him. His cheeks are dark with grime. His eyes look sick and bright.

He goes to a pay phone and calls his mother collect.

"How'd you like to drive to Norton Beach?" he asks her. He explains about the carnival, and that he would like to come home.

"Well, I think it sounds enriching, honestly."

"It's not. Come and get me."

"David has a fractured rib," she says. "It's not all your fault, I know. You're both barbarous idiots, as far as I'm concerned. If I weren't so spineless, I'd tell the two of you to go fly a kite and live out my cronehood in solitude, but so be it. I'm a coward."

"Will you please come and get me?"

"What you ask is impossible. I can't bring you back here."

"Could you wire me some money?"

"Fifty dollars is missing from my purse."

"Forty."

"Ah, my apologies," she says.

"Just get in the car."

The line is silent a moment. She sighs. "Look, I'm sorry, but now isn't a good time. The Hendersons will be here in an hour, and I've got artichokes to stuff. Call me in two or three days, and we can talk things over. But really, I think in a way this could be a good thing. You needed a fire under you, I think."

A young reporter from the *Norton Beach Intelligencer*, on hand to cover the Future Farmers of America duck race, instead assigns himself a story on the accidental staving-in of the Zipper man's head. Gary is in a coma and not expected to return. The reporter, who is not much older than Jeff Park, stops by the pirate ship to harvest a quote or two from those who knew him. He wands the butt of his ballpoint pen at Leon and Jeff, who both decline to speak. But Ellis is keen to talk to the young man. "Gary was a seriously generous person," says Ellis. "That was the main thing about him."

The reporter jots this information down, and then looks back at Ellis with a reptilian smile. "You know what they're selling over at the company office? A few years back Gary pulled a bid in Jackson Correctional for putting his hands on a four-year-old."

He lights a cigarette, savoring his custody of this ugly news about the Zipper man. "Course, they're trying to pin that thing from the other night on him, but to me, there's something about it that doesn't pass the smell test." He inhales a lungful and narrows his eyes at the Chaises Volantes, as though the Chaises Volantes do not pass the smell test, either. Then he goes across the way to Roy's Hoop-La, the basketball toss. The reporter sinks a very respectable three shots out of five, though the hoop is rigged and shaped like a kidney bean.

The FFA beef steer competition is under way in the agriculture pavilion. Chad is there with his black steer. He wears a kelly-green vest and bow tie, like the half-dozen young men and women standing beside him, stroking their animals' bellies with slender hooked sticks.

The judge, Horace Tate, is a man with a kind, boiled-looking face and a striped shirt tight over his prosperous belly. At his command, the contestants lead their animals around the ring in a sober march. After three laps, Tate brushes some sawdust from his cowboy hat and speaks into a microphone. "In judging this competition," he says, "I was looking for the total package: a long-bodied, high-volume steer with good travelability and a masculine look. These young people have brought some very fine animals here tonight, but I think I'm going to have to give the first prize to . . . Chad's Black Brangus, Domino. Chad, how about you say a few words about raising Domino here." In fact, Domino's a little sickle-hocked, but the finest steer, a white Charolais so flawless it looks carved out of soap, is owned by a squirrelly boy with bad acne and an untucked shirt who Tate feels is not a credit to the FFA.

Chad looks fearfully at the microphone. He speaks into it in a voice scarcely louder than a whisper. "He was a pretty slow gainer. He was tough to halter-break."

While Chad murmurs at the empty stands, Horace Tate polishes his belt buckle with the cuff of his shirtsleeve. He's proud of the buckle, a silver oval, studded in the center with a turquoise moon. His daughter was in high school when she made it for him. She lives in Santa Fe now, though he hasn't heard from her in many years. Tate worries over his daughter, but the buckle comforts him, offers some assurance that things will turn out well for her.

The competition ends. Chad leaves with his blue ribbon. The boy with the white steer and rumpled cheeks receives a commendation for keeping the neatest logbook.

Tate's down here for the week. He's got a small ranch two hours west of here, outside Kissimmee, where he runs a few dozen head of skinny cattle and the alpaca herd his wife insists on keeping. In his younger years, Tate rode competition rough stock and then drove race cars, drawn to anything with mind-erasing speed. But he doesn't care for the pointless velocity of the carnival amusements. Looking out at the whirling skyline of the fair, he can't help thinking about all the earth you could move, all the beef you could haul with so much fuel and good steel. He thinks, too, of last night, of the boy in the Honeypot, and feels a pleasant ache, like being rasped on the back of the sternum with a jeweler's file. There's a want in him to take a stroll around, but he pushes it down. Instead, Tate goes to the one ride he enjoys—the Cliff Hanger, a fleet of little hammocks dangling beneath hang gliders' wings. The wing-and-hammock rigs are bolted to a spinning ring of steel that, as it turns, soars high above the midway on a massive hydraulic arm. It is a gentle ride, designed by a large-hearted engineer who valued amazement over stark fear. You lie on your stomach with nothing beneath you. No other ride more perfectly approximates the feeling of bird flight. Up goes the arm. Swooping high and smooth above the fair, Tate giggles helplessly, the night air hitting him like a fast, sweet joke.

"Excuse you, asshole," a biker lady tells Jeff Park. She's wearing a pair of high-dollar boots trimmed with spurs and moto-fringe. In his haste to meet the girl Katie, Jeff Park trod on her toe. But Jeff's gone down the midway. What a funny hunger he's got to see this girl he hasn't shared five minutes' talk with. Katie and her green-lit teeth—he couldn't say why, but she's the first thing that's made any sense since the old man went for him in the sunroom. It's not sexual urgency that hurries him but a kind of giddy fondness. He pictures her bedroom, clean and full of girl smells in a house far from here. The thought gets the saliva pooling under his tongue.

But she's not waiting for him at the coin toss, whose only patrons are two elderly women flinging dimes at dismal bounty—cloudy pilsner glasses, heaps of yellowed T-shirts, coffee mugs bearing obscure slogans—"Beezer County Recycling Program," "Sulphur City Granddad." While the attendant isn't looking, Jeff Park puts the toe of his shoe over three dimes and drags them under the rope.

Fifteen minutes pass, and Katie does not appear. Jeff feels like the victim of a theft. He doesn't find her at the Forty Niner, the trough where, for five dollars, you can pan a sack of rigged dirt prestudded with unprecious gems. No luck either at the Zyklon, the Thunderbolt, the Roundup, the FireBall, or the Starship 2000, or at the toilet line or at the Village of Yesteryear. It's almost ten o'clock when he sees her orange sweater among the throng of taunters at the Bengal tiger cage, watching the great cat stride his unceasing laps. Jeff calls her name. She is laughing at something the girl next to her is saying, and doesn't hear. He goes to her quickly, puts his hand on her shoulder, and pulls her toward him, hard enough that her head jerks back. People turn. Her jaw hangs wide and pretty, but the light in her mouth has gone out.

EVERYTHING
RAVAGED,
EVERYTHING
BURNED

Just as we were all getting back into the mainland domestic groove, somebody started in with dragons and crop blights from across the North Sea. We all knew who it was. A turncoat Norwegian monk named Naddod had been big medicine on the dragon-and-blight circuit for the last decade or so, and was known to bring heavy ordnance for whoever could lay out some silver. Scuttlebutt had it that Naddod was operating out of a monastery on Lindisfarne, whose people we'd troubled on a pillage-and-consternation tour through Northumbria after Corn Harvesting Month last fall. Now bitter winds were screaming in from the west, searing the land and ripping the grass from the soil. Salmon were turning up spattered with sores, and grasshoppers clung to the wheat in rapacious buzzing bunches.

I tried to put these things out of my mind. We'd been away three long months harrying the Hibernian shores, and now I was back with Pila, my common-law, and thinking that home was very close to paradise in these endless summer days. We'd built our house together, Pila and me. It was a fine little wattle-and-daub cabin on a pretty bit of plain where a wide blue fjord stabbed into the land. On summer evenings my young wife and I would sit out front, high on potato wine, and watch the sun stitch its orange skirt across the horizon. At times such as these, you get a good, humble feeling, like the gods made this place, this moment, first and concocted you as an afterthought just to be there to enjoy it.

I was doing a lot of enjoying and relishing and laying around the rack with Pila, though I knew what it meant when I heard those flint-edged winds howling past the house. Some individuals three weeks' boat ride off were messing up our summer and would probably need their asses whipped over it.

Of course, Djarf Fairhair had his stinger out even before his wife spotted those dragons winging it inland from the coast. He was boss on our ship and a fool for warfare. His appetite for action was so terrifying and infectious, he'd once riled up a gang of Frankish slaves and led them south to afflict and maim their own countrymen. He'd gotten in four days of decent sacking when the slaves began to see the situation for what it was and underwent a sudden change of attitude. Djarf had been fighting his way up the Rhine Valley, making steady progress through a half-assed citizens' militia of children and farmers, when the slaves closed in behind him. People who were there say he turned absolutely feral and began berserking with a pair of broadaxes, chewing through the lines like corn kernels on a cob, and that when the axes broke, he took up someone's severed leg and used it as a club, so horrifying those gentle provincials that they fell back and gave him wide berth to the ship.

Djarf was from Hedeby-Slesvig up the Sli fjord, a foul and rocky locality whose people take a worrisome pleasure in the gruesome sides of life. They have a habit down there if they don't like a child's looks when he slides from the womb, they pitch him into the deep and wait for the next one. Djarf himself was supposedly a colicky baby, and it was only the beneficence of the tides and his own vicious tenacity that got him to the far beach when his father tried to wash him from the world.

He'd been campaigning for payback ever since. I guess I was with him on a search-and-destroy tour against Louis the Pious, and with my own eyes watched him climb up over the soldiers' backs and stride across their shoulders, scything skulls as he went. On that same trip, we ran low on food, and it was Djarf who decided to throw our own dead on the fire and have at last night's mutton when their stomachs burst. He'd been the only one of us to dig in, apart from a deranged Arab along as a spell-buster. He reached right in there, scooping out chewed-up victuals with a shank of pine bark. "Greenhorns," he called us, the firelight twitching on his face. "Food's food. If these boys hadn't gotten their threads snipped, they'd tell you the same thing."

So Djarf, whose wife was a sour, carp-mouthed thing and lit-tle argument for staying home, was agitating to hop back in the ship and go straighten things out in Northumbria. My buddy Gnut, who lived just over the stony moraine our wheat field backed up on, came down the hill one day and admitted that he, too, was giving it some thought. Like me, he wasn't big on war-rioring. He was just crazy for boat. He'd have rowed from his shack to his shithouse if somebody would invent a ship whose prow could cut sod. His wife had passed years ago, dead from bad milk, and now that she was gone, the part of Gnut that felt peaceful in a place that didn't move beneath him had sickened and died as well.

Pila saw him coming down the hill and scowled. "Don't need to guess what he'll be wanting," she said, and headed back indoors. Gnut ambled down over the hummocky earth and stopped at the pair of stump chairs Pila and I had put up on the hill where the view was so fine. From there, the fjord shone like poured silver, and sometimes you could spot a seal poking his head up through the waves.

Gnut's wool coat was stiff with filth and his long hair so heavy and unclean that even the raw wind was having a hard time getting it to move. He had a good crust of snot going in his mustache, not a pleasant thing to look at, but then, he had no one around to find it disagreeable. He tore a sprig of heather from the ground and chewed at its sweet roots.

"Djarf get at you yet?" he asked.

"No, not yet, but I'm not worried he'll forget."

He took the sprig from his teeth and briefly jammed it into his ear before tossing it away. "You gonna go?"

"Not until I hear the particulars, I won't."

"You can bet I'm going. A hydra flew in last night and ran off Rolf Hierdal's sheep. We can't be putting up with this shit. It comes down to pride, is what it comes down to."

"Hell, Gnut, when'd you get to be such a gung-ho mother-fucker? I don't recall you being so proud and thin-skinned before Astrud went off to her good place. Anyhow, Lindisfarne is probably sacked-out already. If you don't recall, we pillaged the tar out of those people on the last swing through, and I doubt they've come up with much in the meantime to justify a trip."

I wished Gnut would go ahead and own up to the fact that his life out here was making him lonely and miserable instead of laying on with this warrior-man routine. I could tell just to look at him that most days he was thinking of walking into the water and not bothering to turn back. It wasn't combat he was after. He wanted back on the boat among company.

Not that I was all that averse to a job myself, speaking in the abstract, but I was needing more sweet time with Pila. I cared more for that girl than even she probably knew, and I was hoping to get in some thorough lovemaking before the Haycutting

Month was under way and see if I couldn't make us a little monkey.

But the days wore on and the weather worsened. Pila watched it closely, and the sadness welled up in her, as it often did when I'd be leaving. She cussed me on some days, and others she'd hold me to her and weep. And late one evening, far toward dawn, the hail started. It came suddenly, with the rasping sound a ship makes when its keel scrapes stone. We hunkered down in the sheepskins, and I whispered soothing things to Pila, trying to drown out the clatter.

The sun was not yet full up in the sky when Djarf came and knocked. I rose and stepped across the floor, which was damp with cold dew. Djarf stood in the doorway wearing a mail jacket and shield and breathing like he'd jogged the whole way over. He chucked a handful of hail at my feet. "Today's the day," he said with a wild grin. "We got to get it on."

Sure, I could have told him thanks anyway, but once you back down from one job, you're lucky if they'll even let you put in for a flat-fee trade escort. I had to think long-term, me and Pila, and any little jits we might produce. Still, she didn't like to hear it. When I got back in bed, she tucked the covers over her face, hoping I'd think she was angry instead of crying.

The clouds were spilling out low across the sky when we shoved off. Thirty of us on board, Gnut rowing with me at the bow and behind us a lot of other men I'd been in some shit with before. Some of their families came down to watch us go. Ørl Stender fucked up the cadence waving to his son, who stood on the beach waving back. He was a tiny one, not four or five, standing there with no pants on, holding a baby pig on a hide leash. Some of the others on board weren't a whole lot older, rash and violent children, so innocent about the world they would just as soon stick a knife in you as shake your hand.

Gnut was overjoyed. He laughed and sang and put a lot of muscle into the oar, me just holding my hands on it to keep up appearances. I was missing Pila already. I watched the beach for her and her bright red hair. She hadn't come down to see me off, too mad and sad about me leaving to get up out of bed. But I looked for her anyway, the land scooting away with every jerk of the oars. If Gnut knew I was hurting, he didn't say so. He nudged me and joked, and kept up a steady flow of dull, merry chatter, as though this whole thing was a private vacation the two of us had cooked up together.

Djarf stood at his spot in the bow, the blood in his cheeks. His high spirits were wearying. Slesvigers will burst into song with no provocation whatever, their affinity for music roughly on a par with the wretchedness of their singing. He screeched out a cadence ballad that lasted hours, and his gang of young hockchoppers howled along with him and gave no one any peace.

Three days out, the sun punched through the dirty clouds and put a steely shimmer on the sea. It cooked the brine out of our clothes and got everybody dry and happy. I couldn't help but think that if Naddod was really as serious as we thought he was, this crossing would be a fine opportunity to call up a typhoon and drown us all like cats. But the weather held, and the seas stayed drowsy and low.

We had less light in the evenings out here than at home, and it was a little easier sleeping in the open boat without an all-night sun. Gnut and I slept where we rowed, working around each other to get comfy on the bench. I woke up once in the middle of the night and found Gnut dead asleep, muttering and slobbering and holding me in a rough embrace. I tried to peel him off, but he was large, and his hard arms stayed on me tight as if they'd grown there. I poked him and yelled at him, but the big man would not be roused, so I just tried to work up a little slack to where he wasn't hurting my ribs, and I drifted back to sleep.

Later, I told him what had happened. "That's a lot of horse-shit," he said, his broad face going red.

"I wish it was," I said. "But I've got bruises I could show you. Hey, if I ever come around asking to be your sweetheart, do me a favor and remind me about last night."

He was all upset. "Go to hell, Harald. You're not funny. No-body thinks you're funny."

"I'm sorry," I said. "Guess you haven't had a whole lot of practice lately having a body beside you at night."

He rested on the oar a second. "So what if I haven't."

Thanks to the easy wind bellying our sails, we crossed fast and sighted the island six days early. One of the hockchoppers spot-ted it first, and when he did, he let everyone know it by cutting loose with a long, obnoxious battle howl. He drew his sword and swung it in figure eights above his head, causing the men around him to scatter under the gunwales. This boy was a nasty item, with a face like a buzzard's, his cheeks showing more boils than beard. I'd seen him around at home. He had three blackened, chopped-off thumbs reefed to his belt.

Haakon Gokstad glanced up from his seat in the stern and shot the boy a baleful look. Haakon had been on more raids and runs than the bunch of us put together. He was old and achy and worked the rudder, partly because he could read the tides by how the blood moved through his hands, and also because those old arms were poor for pulling oars. "Put your ass on that bench, young man," Haakon said to the boy. "We got twelve hours' work between here and there."

The boy colored. He let his sword arm hang. He looked at his friends to see if he'd been humiliated in front of them and, if he had, what he needed to do about it. The whole boat was looking over him. Even Djarf paused in his song. The other kid on his bench whispered something and scooted over. The boy sat and took the oar. The rowing and the chatter started up again.

You could say that those people on Lindisfarne were fools, living out there on a tiny island without high cliffs or decent natural defenses, and so close to us and also the Swedes and the Norwegians, how we saw it, we couldn't afford *not* to come by and sack every now and again. But when we came into the bright little bay, a quiet fell over all of us. Even the hockchoppers quit grab-assing and looked. The place was wild with fields of purple thistle, and when the wind blew, it twitched and rolled, like the hide of some fantastic animal shrugging in its sleep. Wildflowers spurted on the hills in fat red gouts. Apple trees lined the shore, and there was something sorrowful in how they hung so low with fruit. We could see a man making his way toward a clump of white-walled cottages, his donkey loping along behind him with a load. On the far hill, I could make out the silhouette of the monastery, which still lacked a roof from when we'd burned it last. It was a lovely place, and I hoped there would still be something left to enjoy after we got off the ship and wrecked it up.

We gathered on the beach, and already Djarf was in a lather. He did a few deep knee bends, got down in front of all of us and ran through some poses, cracking his bones and drawing out the knots in his muscles. Then he closed his eyes and said a silent prayer. His eyes were still closed when a man in a long robe appeared, picking his way down through the thistle.

Haakon Gokstad had a finger stuck in his mouth where one of his teeth had come out. He removed the finger and spat through the hole. He nodded up the hill at the figure heading our way, "My, that sumbitch has got some brass," he said.

The man walked straight to Djarf. He stood before him and removed his hood. His hair lay thin on his scalp and had probably been blond before it went white. He was old, with lines on his face that could have been drawn with a dagger point.

"Naddod," Djarf said, dipping his head slightly. "Suppose you've been expecting us."

"I certainly have not," Naddod said. He brought his hand up to the rude wooden cross that hung from his neck. "And I won't sport with you and pretend the surprise is entirely a pleasant one. Frankly, there isn't much left here worth pirating, so, yes, it's a bit of a puzzle."

"Uh-huh," said Djarf. "Can't tell us anything about a hailstorm, or locusts and shit, or a bunch of damn dragons coming around and scaring the piss out of everybody's wife. You don't know nothing about any of that."

Naddod held his palms up and smiled piteously. "No, I'm very sorry, I don't. We did send a monkey pox down to the Spanish garrison at Much Wenlock, but honestly, nothing your way."

Djarf's tone changed, and his voice got loud and amiable. "Huh. Well, that's something." He turned to us and held up his hands. "Hey, boys, hate to break it to you, but it sounds like somebody fucked something up here. Old Naddod says it wasn't him, and as soon as he tells me just who in the hell it was behind the inconveniences we been having, we'll get back under way."

"Right." Naddod was uneasy, and I could see a chill run

through him. "If you're passing through Mercia, I know they've just gotten hold of this man Aethelrik. Supposed to be a very tough customer. You know, that was his leprosy outbreak last year in—"

Djarf was grinning and nodding, but Naddod looked suddenly ill.

Djarf kept a small knife in his belt, and in the way other men smoked a pipe or chewed seeds, Djarf liked to strop that little knife. It was sharpened down to a little fingernail of blade. You could shave a fairy's ass with that thing. And while Naddod was talking, Djarf had pulled out his knife and drawn it neatly down the priest's belly. At the sight of blood washing over the white seashells, everybody pressed forward, hollering and whipping their swords around. Djarf was overcome with crazed elation, and he hopped up and down, yelling for everybody to be quiet and watch him.

Naddod was not dead. His insides had pretty much spilled out, but he was still breathing. Not crying out or anything, though, which you had to give him credit for. Djarf hunkered and flipped Naddod onto his stomach and rested a foot in the small of his back.

Gnut was right beside me. He sighed and put his hand over his eyes. "Oh, Lord, he doing a blood eagle?"

"Yeah," I said. "Looks that way."

Djarf raised his palm for quiet. "Now I know most of the old-timers have seen one of these, but it might be a new one on some of you young men." The hockchoppers tittered. "This thing is what we call a blood *eagle*, and if you'll just sit tight a second you can see—well, it's a pretty wild effect."

The men stepped back to give Djarf room to work. He placed the point of his sword to one side of Naddod's spine. He leaned into it and worked the steel in gingerly, delicately crunching through one rib at a time until he'd made an incision about a foot long. He paused to wipe sweat from his brow, and made a parallel cut on the other side of the backbone. Then he knelt and put his hands into the cuts. He fumbled around in there a second, and then drew Naddod's lungs out through the slits. As Naddod huffed and gasped, the lungs flapped, looking sort of like a pair of wings. I had to turn away myself. It was very grisly stuff.

The young men roared, and Djarf stood there, conducting the applause. Then, at his command, they all broke out their sieging tackle and swarmed up the hill.

Only Gnut and Haakon and Ørl Stender and me didn't go. Ørl watched the others flock up toward the monastery, and when he was sure no one was looking back, he went to where Naddod lay dying, and struck him hard on the skull with the back of a hatchet. We were all relieved to see those lungs stop quivering. Ørl sighed and blessed himself. He said a funerary prayer, the gist of which was that he didn't know what this man's god was all about, but he was sorry that his humble servant had gotten sent up early, and on a bullshit pretext, too. He said he didn't know the man, but that he probably deserved something better the next time around.

"Cross all that water for this damn stupidity, and a flock of sheep to shave at home," Haakon grumbled.

Gnut smiled and squinted up at the sky. "My God, it's a fine day. Let's go up the hill and see if we can't scratch up a bite to eat."

We hiked to the little settlement on the hill. Some ways over, where the monastery was, the young men were on a real binge. They'd dragged out a half-dozen monks, hanged them from a tree, and then set the tree on fire.

Our hands were stiff and raw from the row over, and we paused at a well in the center of the village to wet our palms and have a drink. We were surprised to see the kid with the thumbs in his belt bust forth from a stand of ash trees, yanking some poor half-dead citizen along behind him. He walked over to where we were standing and let his victim collapse in the dusty boulevard.

"This is nice," he said to us. "You'd make good chieftains, standing around like this, watching other people work."

"Why, you little turd," Haakon said, and backhanded the boy across the mouth. The fellow lying there in the dust looked up and chuckled. The boy flushed. He plucked a dagger from his hip scabbard and stabbed Haakon in the stomach. There was a still moment. Haakon gazed down at the ruby stain spreading across his tunic. He looked greatly vexed.

As the young man realized what he'd done, his features fretted up like a child trying to pout his way out of a spanking. He was still looking that way when Haakon cleaved his head across the eyebrows with one crisp stroke.

Haakon cleaned his sword and looked again at his stomach. "Sumbitch," he said, probing the wound with his pinky. "It's deep. I believe I'm in a fix."

"Nonsense," said Gnut. "Just need to lay you down and stitch you up."

Ørl, who was softhearted, went over to the man the youngster had left. He propped him up against the well and gave him the bucket to sip at.

Across the road, an old dried-up farmer had come out of his house. He stared off at the smoke from the monastery rolling down across the bay. He nodded at us. We walked over.

"Hello," he said.

I told him good day.

He squinted at my face. "Something wrong?" I asked him.

"Apologies," he said. "Just thought I recognized you, is all."

"Could be. I was through here last fall."

"Uh-huh," he said. "Now, that was a hot one. Don't know why you'd want to come back. You got everything that was worth a damn on the last going-over."

"Yeah, well, we're having a hard time figuring it ourselves. Came to see your man Naddod. Wrong guy, looks like, but he got gotten anyway, sorry to say."

The man sighed. "Doesn't harelip me any. We all had to tithe in to cover his retainer. Do just as well without him, I expect. So what are you doing, any looting?"

"Why? You got anything to loot?"

"Me? Oh, no. Got a decent cookstove, but I can't see you toting that back on the ship."

"Don't suppose you've got a coin hoard or anything buried out back?"

"Jeezum crow, I wish I did have. Coin hoard, I'd really turn things around for myself."

"Yeah, well, I don't suppose you'd own up if you did."

He laughed. "You got that right, my friend. But I suppose you got to kill me or believe me, and either way, you get nothing out of the deal." He pointed at Haakon, who was leaning on Gnut and looking pretty spent. "Looks like your friend's got a problem. Unless you'd like to watch him die, why don't you bring him inside? Got a daughter who's hell's own seamstress."

The man, who was called Bruce, had a cozy little place. We all filed in. His daughter was standing by the stove. She gave a nervous little cry when we came through the door. She had a head full of thick black hair, and a thin face, pale as sugar— a pretty girl. So pretty, in fact, that you didn't notice right off that she was missing an arm. We all balked and had a good stare at her. But Gnut, you could tell, was truly smitten. The way he looked, blanched and wide-eyed, he could have been facing a wild dog instead of a good-looking woman. He rucked his hands through his hair and tried to lick the crust off his lips. Then he nodded and uttered a solemn "Hullo."

"Mary," Bruce said, "this man has developed a hole in his stomach. I said we'd help fix him up."

Mary looked at Haakon. "Aha," she said. She lifted his tunic and surveyed the wound. "Water," she said to Ørl, who was looking on. Gnut eyed him jealously as he left for the well. Then Gnut cleared his throat. "I'd like to pitch in," he said. Mary directed him to a little sack of onions in the corner and told him to chop. Bruce got a fire going in the stove. Mary set the water on and shook in some dry porridge. Haakon, who had grown rather waxen, crawled up on the table and lay still. "I don't feel like no porridge," he said.

"Don't worry about that," Bruce said. "The porridge is just for the onions to ride in on."

Gnut kept an eye on Mary as he bent over a small table and overdid it on the onions. He chopped and chopped, and when he'd chopped all they had, he started chopping the chopped-up ones over again. Finally, Mary looked over and told him, "That's fine, thank you," and Gnut laid the knife down.

When the porridge was cooked, Mary threw in a few handfuls of onion and took the concoction over to Haakon. He regarded her warily, but when she held the wooden spoon out to him, he opened his mouth like a baby bird. He chewed and swallowed. "Doesn't taste very good," he said, but he kept eating anyway.

A minute passed, and then a peculiar thing occurred. Mary lifted Haakon's tunic again, put her face to the wound, and sniffed at it. She paused a second and then did it again.

"What in the world is this?" I asked.

"Gotta do this with a wound like that," Bruce said. "See if he's got the porridge illness."

"He doesn't have any porridge illness," I said. "At least, he didn't before now. What he's got is a stab hole in his stomach. Now stitch the man up."

"Won't do any good if you smell onions coming out of that hole. Means he's got the porridge illness and he's done for."

Haakon looked up. "Talking about a pierced bowel? Can't believe it's as bad as all that."

Mary had another sniff. The wound didn't smell like onions. She cleaned Haakon with hot water and stitched the hole to a tight pucker.

Haakon fingered the stitches, and, satisfied, passed out. The five of us stood around, and no one could think of anything to say.

"So," Gnut said in an offhand way. "Were you born like that?"

"Like what?" Mary said.

"Without both arms, I mean. Is that how you came out?"

"Sir, that's fine a thing to ask my daughter," Bruce said. "It was your people that did it to her."

Gnut said, "Oh." And then he said it again, and then really no one could think of anything to say.

Then Mary spoke. "It wasn't you who did it," she said. "But the man who did, I think I'd like to kill him."

Gnut told her that if she would please let him know who it was, he'd consider it a favor if she'd let him intervene on her behalf.

I said, "I would like a drink. Ørl, what have you got in that wineskin?"

He said nothing. The skin hung from his shoulder, and he put his hands on it protectively.

"I asked what have you got to drink."

"Little bit of root brandy, for your information, Harald. But it's got to last me the way back. I can't be damp and not have something to take the chill off."

Gnut was glad to have something to raise his voice about. "Ørl, you're a sonofabitch. We been three weeks on the water for nothing, Haakon is maybe gonna die, and you can't even see your way to splash a little taste around. Now, that is the worst, the lowest thing I've ever heard."

So Ørl opened up his wineskin, and we all had a dose. It was sweet and potent and we drank and laughed and carried on. Haakon came to. His ordeal had put him in a mawkish bent of mind, and he raised a toast to his pretty surgeon, and to the splendid day, and how much it pleased him that he'd get to see the end of it. Bruce and Mary loosened up and we all talked like old friends. Mary told a lewd story about an apothecary who lived down the road. She was having a good time and did not seem to mind how close Gnut was standing. No one looking in on us would have known we were the reason this girl was missing an arm, and also the reason, probably, that nobody asked where Bruce's wife had gone.

It was not long before we heard somebody causing a commotion at the well. Me and Gnut and Ørl stepped outside. Djarf had stripped to his waist, and his face and arms and pants looked about how you'd figure. He was hauling up buckets of cold water, dumping it over his head, and shrieking with delight. The blood ran off him pink and watery. He saw us and came over.

"Hoo," he said, shaking water from his hair. He jogged in place for a minute, shivered, and then straightened up. "Mercy, that was a spree. Not much loot to speak of, but a hell of a god-damn spree." He massaged his thighs and spat a few times. Then he said, "So, you do much killing?"

"Nah," I said. "Haakon killed that little what's-his-name lying over there, but no, we've just been sort of taking it easy."

"Hm. What about in there?" he asked, indicating Bruce's cottage. "Who lives there? You kill them?"

"No, we didn't," Ørl said. "They helped put Haakon back together and everything. Seem like good folks."

"Nobody's killing them," Gnut said.

"So everybody's back at the monastery, then?" I asked.

"Well, most of them. Those young men had a disagreement over some damn thing and fell to cutting each other. Gonna make for a tough row out of here. Pray for wind, I guess."

Brown smoke was heavy in the sky, and I could hear dim sounds of people screaming.

"So here's the deal," Djarf said. "We bivouac here tonight, and if the weather holds, we shoot down to Mercia tomorrow and see if we can't sort things out with this fucker Aethelrik."

"I don't know," Ørl said.

"No deal," I said. "This thing was a goose chase as it is. I got a wife at home and wheat straw to bale. I'll be damned if I'll row you to Mercia."

Djarf clenched his jaw. He looked at Gnut. "You, too?"

Gnut nodded.

"Serious? Mutiny?"

"No," Gnut said. "We're just saying we—"

"Call it what it is, motherfucker," Djarf barked. "You sons of bitches are mutinizing my operation?"

"Look, Djarf," I said. "Nobody's doing anything to anybody. We just need to head on back."

He yelled and snorted. Then he ran at us with his sword raised high, and Gnut had to slip behind him quickly and put a bear hug on him. I went over and clamped one hand over Djarf's mouth and pinched his nose shut with the other, and after a while he started to cool down.

We let him go. He stood there huffing and eyeing us, and we kept our knives and things out, and finally he put the sword back and composed himself.

"Okay, sure, I read you," he said. "Fair enough. We go back. Oh, I should have told you, Olaffssen found a stash of beef shells somewhere. He's gonna cook those up for everybody who's left. Ought to be tasty." He turned and humped it back toward the bay.

Gnut didn't come down to the feast. He said he needed to stay at Bruce and Mary's to look after Haakon. Bullshit, of course, seeing as Haakon made it down the hill by himself and crammed his tender stomach with about nine tough steaks. When the dusk started going black and still no Gnut, I legged it back up to Bruce's to see about him. Gnut was sitting on a hollow log outside the cottage, flicking gravel into the weeds.

"She's coming with me," he said.

"Mary?"

He nodded gravely. "I'm taking her home with me to be my wife. She's in there talking it over with Bruce."

"This a voluntary thing, or an abduction-type deal?"

Gnut looked off toward the bay as though he hadn't heard the question. "She's coming with me."

I mulled it over. "You sure this is such a hot idea, bringing her back to live among our people, all things considering?"

He grew quiet. "Any man that touches her, or says anything unkind, it will really be something different, what I'll do to him."

We sat a minute and watched the sparks rising from the bonfire on the beach. The warm evening wind carried smells of blossoms and wood smoke, and I was overcome with calm.

We walked into Bruce's, where only a single suet candle was going. Mary stood by the window with her one arm across her chest. Bruce was worked up. When we came in, he moved to block the door. "You get out of my house," he said. "You just can't take her, what little I've got."

Gnut did not look happy, but he shouldered past and

knocked Bruce on his ass. I went and put a hand on the old farmer, who was quaking with rage.

Mary did not hold her hand out to Gnut. But she didn't protest when he put his arm around her and moved her toward the door. The look she gave her father was a wretched thing, but still she went easy. With just one arm like that, what could she do? What other man would have her?

Their backs were to us when Bruce grabbed up an awl from the table and made for Gnut. I stepped in front of him and broke a chair on his face, but still he kept coming, scrabbling at my sword, trying to snatch up something he could use to keep his daughter from going away. I had to hold him steady and run my knife into his cheek. I held it there like a horse's bit, and then he didn't want to move. When I got up off him he was crying quietly. As I was leaving, he threw something at me and knocked the candle out.

And you might think it was a good thing, that Gnut had found a woman who would let him love her, and if she didn't exactly love him back, at least she would, in time, get to feeling something for him that wasn't so far from it. But what would you say about that crossing, when the winds went slack and it was five long weeks before we finally fetched up home? Gnut didn't hardly say a word to anybody, just held Mary close to him, trying to keep her soothed and safe from all of us, his friends. He wouldn't look me in the face, stricken as he was by the awful fear that comes with getting hold of something you can't afford to lose.

After that trip, things changed. It seemed to me that all of us were leaving the high and easy time of life and heading into deeper waters. Not long after we got back, Djarf had a worm crawl up a hole in his foot and had to give up raiding. Gnut and

Mary turned to homesteading full-time, and I saw less of him. Just catching up over a jar turned into a hassle you had to plan two weeks in advance. And when we did get together, he would laugh and jaw with me a little bit, but you could see he had his mind on other things. He'd gotten what he wanted, but he didn't seem too happy about it, just worried all the time.

It didn't make much sense to me then, what Gnut was going through, but after Pila and me had our little twins, and we put a family together, I got an understanding of how terrible love can be. You wish you hated those people, your wife and children, because you know the things the world will do to them, because you have done some of those things yourself. It's crazy-making, yet you cling to them with everything and close your eyes against the rest of it. But still you wake up late at night and lie there listening for the creak and splash of oars, the clank of steel, the sounds of men rowing toward your home.

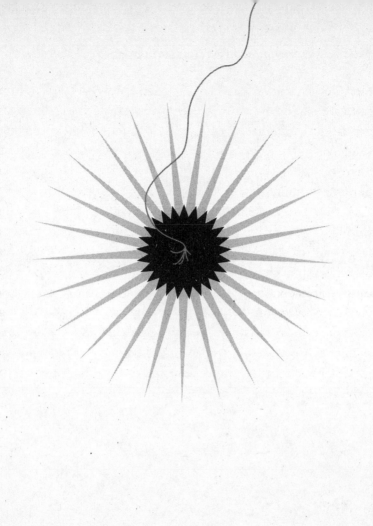

Acknowledgments

Thank you:

Ben Austen, Jack Bookman, Joe Bookman, Willing Davidson, Betsy Dawson, Marion Duvert, Harrison Haynes, Courtney Hodell, Eli Horowitz, Brigid Hughes, George Jenne, Matt Jones, Mark Krotov, the MacDowell Colony, Ben Marcus, Madeline Neal, the New Orleans Center for Creative Arts, David Rowell, Amanda Schoonmaker, Heather Schroder, Ed Tower, Lauren Wilcox, the Corporation of Yaddo.